SWITCH

B. A. PAUL

For Lois.
Thanks for believing in me...

PROLOGUE

FLAMES LICK his arms as he stirs the molten brass. He's used to the heat. It's like an old friend.

Never wavering.

Always present.

He pours the magical metallic liquid into the mold and allows the brass to fill every corner. He watches the liquid closely to be sure there are no bubbles or mistakes. A simple design, really. Vines twisting with strands of life. In memory of those who'd gone before. Who didn't yet know how to harness the restless magic inside of them.

For those who didn't quite know what they were.

But he knew. And he knew how to slow down the internal erosion. To keep the magical power burning brightly enough to be useful, but not so bright that it consumed the bits of his kind that remained…human.

Once satisfied with his work, he sets the mold aside to cool and glances around his workshop lit by only the kiln's flame. To the untrained eye, his space looks like any other blacksmith or cobbler shop. Rows of tables and tools of all sorts and sizes hang from the walls and wooden ceiling beams. He'd covered the windows with heavy burlap to keep out the light.

And the sneaks.

One table, far away from the flames of the kiln, holds notebooks of heavy parchment pages sewn with thin strips of brown leather, carefully filled with scrolling artwork, sketches, and lists of ingredients in just the right amounts. Many notebooks serve as a master catalog, listing the items he and his father had forged in fire over decades.

On the other wooden table, bits and pieces of cogs, wheels, gears, and switches line up just so. Levers and pulleys of all shapes and sizes. When the flames leap from the kiln in just the right way, he can make out the glistening green and blue of…specialness. Bits and drips and drops of magic worked into each iron and steel and brass creation with the utmost attention to detail.

Some designs boast roses for his sister. In others he etched daisies for his mother. On some he put both, the petals and leaves twisting in the vines. The clockwork bits, of course, were in honor of his father who seemed to transcend time itself until *they* found him out.

A simple remembrance for the fallen ones. To respect and honor for all time.

In the far corner of the workshop sits a large bassinet made from twisted branches, vines, and rope and lined with green velvet from the skirt of his wife's favorite dress. Faint cries of hunger from the boy pull him from his work.

He walks over and looks down on his *other* creations. The most important ones of all.

"Hello, Knox, my son. One day this duty will be yours." He rubs the baby's forehead and Knox calms, staring up at him with *knowing*.

With understanding.

"And hello, my sweet one. Dear Kuri." He brushed his infant daughter's forehead. "You. *You* will be his helper!"

CHAPTER 1

THE JUNE SUN sizzles on my neck as the antique tractor sputters among the rows of corn. I know I'm too old to ride alongside Granddad on this rickety machine. The farmers on either side of Granddad's land own newer equipment with air conditioning and satellite radios.

But not Granddad.

I always enjoy our time together, though, despite Granddad's quirks. Even if it means riding with my right foot on the rusty wheel hub and the left bent awkwardly behind Granddad's leg. I balance with one hand bracing the back of the seat (now covered in its tenth layer of green duct tape) and the other hand on the steering wheel to keep from being jarred off into the corn.

Granddad always steers though. Always.

"School will be out soon. What'cha gonna do over the break, Oliver?" Granddad shouts over the tractor's engine.

"This. I like doing this," I shout back.

It's not windy today, or I'd not be allowed to ride along since we are spraying the weeds at the field's edges. If the slightest breeze were present, it would waft the chemicals into our faces as we change directions. "Probably won't kill you, but let's not chance it," would be the excuse to put off the spraying—or for me not to go along.

But today, the early summer air is dead and heavy with humidity.

This past school term had been bizarre. Extreme weather in the region forced the schools to take a year-round schedule to avoid making up snow days for all eternity. This year, in addition to the blizzard in November, massive heat and rain started in late February, spurring the farmers to chance planting their crops earlier than ever before—so early that the corn is already higher than my head.

I breathe deeply and take in the view from the top of the west field. The land rolls and flows along the tree lines and the small creek in the distance. Every year, Granddad leaves wide swaths of unplanted ground. I used to think he left these random paths for the tractor to go between the fields.

So we could take rides together.

But no respectable farmer would give up that much acreage to simple grass paths—the lanes are strategically planned for irrigation and drainage. Turns out nothing about farming is as random as it looks.

Tall, luscious grass would be knee-high before Granddad would hook up the mower attachment to the tractor and slice it down. I often walk the paths, but someone—usually Granddad—always calls me back before I get too far.

They always worry about me. Even now. In eighth grade.

"Glad you love this Son, but you need a life." Granddad's booming voice brings my attention back to the pain in my hip as I struggle to balance on the bobbing tractor.

"I'll probably hang out with Hedge."

"Hedge is strange. Don't you have any normal friends?"

I don't even consider myself to be normal. And I certainly don't have *friends* in the plural sense of the word. In the five years since my family had moved here, I'd only grown close to Hedge. Strange kid. Strange name. I called him by his given name once, and Hedge flipped his gourd. That was the last time I uttered "Walter."

"I like spending time with you." I try unsuccessfully to stretch a kink from between my shoulder blades. "Why don't we ever tend the east field?"

Granddad grins and slaps my shoulder, nearly knocking me into the weeds. "I do that side early in the morning while you're at school. The terrain is rough, and it would bounce you right off under the tires."

I can't imagine how one portion of the field could be any rougher than another. Granddad and his ancestors had farmed this land for over a century, though, and I suspect he knows where all the rough spots are. Unlike the rest of my family, who could care less about tractors, lanes, or rough spots. My family's specialty is creating rough terrain with their drama. Always with the drama.

Dad had broken the generations'-long love of the land. At one time, I'd wished all three of us could farm it together. But Dad hates field work.

And Mom, well, she'd been ready to hitch a ride back to Chicago two years ago.

I have a habit of wishing for things that will never happen.

"'Bout done for today," Granddad says. We could see the farmhouse roof peeking over the corn in the distance. "Shouldn't need another spraying until later this summer."

I nod. "I'll miss being in the field."

"Well, there's no reason to come out this far until then. You know the dangers." Granddad steers the tractor toward the house, and I readjust my grip and footing.

Ever since preschool—since before we moved here—my visits to Granddad's farm carried heavy warnings about the dangers of the corn: The leaves of the fresh, young stalks slice the skin like razor blades. You'll get lost in no time flat. Wild dogs hide in the stalks, waiting to chew your toes off.

Every spring it was the same warning: Don't go into the corn. Once in a while, Granddad planted soybeans or wheat, but he still gave the same, stern lecture, only he'd change the name of the crop. And sometimes he'd change up the sharped-tooth species waiting, lurking, craving a chunk of my flesh.

I heeded those warnings. Mostly.

As I grew, I knew the wild dog thing wasn't so accurate. Getting lost, though, that *was* accurate. I'd read true stories in the newspaper, and, on several occasions, Granddad had gotten called out in the middle of the night—or off the tractor in the middle of the day—to help search for some little kid or city slicker who'd gotten turned around in a field and needed rescue.

So I never went *too* far into the rows.

Sometimes I walk the grassy irrigation lanes when no one is around. The peace and solitude—especially after Mom and Dad have a ruckus—are welcome. And the countryside is such a stark change from the sirens and hustle of the city we'd left behind.

When we reach the barn, I jump down from the wheel hub and Granddad pulls the tractor in for the night. The machine is as old as time, and I'm sure Granddad will continue to piece it together until he can't find parts anymore.

"Gonna go feed the chickens." I grab the feed bucket and start for the coop.

"Hold on there." Granddad motions me back to the barn. "You know, I meant what I said about this summer. I need your help around here, but I want you to have fun, too. You've got the rest of your life to work. Play while you can."

The word "play" sounds funny. I'm too old to play unless it's video games. I wish people would treat me like a middle schooler instead of a kindergartener. But ever since the incident with Billy, the family treats me differently. Weak and frail, only able to handle little bits of change or stress at a time.

I rub my collar bone. It still aches.

Sometimes I wonder if they're right.

Granddad's worry about my happiness unsettles me. He's never been so talkative about such things.

"Love you, Oliver."

"Love you too, Granddad."

I turn to leave the barn, looking back in time to see Granddad wipe a tear away. I hurry out, pretending not to notice. I've never seen

Granddad cry—not even after Granny passed. My stomach hurts now. All of the sudden.

I glance back again, almost afraid to look. Granddad stands in the doorway of the barn, staring out to the east. I follow his gaze, and, for a moment, I think I see a faint, green flicker on the horizon dancing between corn tops and sky. Granddad catches me staring and booms, "Get on to those chickens. You've not got all night."

I forget the flicker and run toward the hungry birds waiting in the coop and a mountain of homework waiting for me upstairs.

But I hang on to the worry of what's got Granddad all worked up.

CHAPTER 2

EARL DREW his tattered oak walking cane onto the floorboard of the car and slammed the door. Another fruitless search. He turned on the AC, and his beard split down the middle from the stale, forced air. He reached for his cigar but thought better of it.

He pulled from the antique store's lot and headed to the next destination. The flea markets were in full swing after the unsavory winter. There'd be many more events through the summer, but Earl found the best pieces early in the season and very early in the mornings.

He was running late today, though. The shop's owner had been overly talkative, and he didn't want to be rude, so he'd listened to her drone on about her grandchildren and her family's vacation plans. Earl hated small talk, but he needed to remain on her good side in case she found any truly unique items. He wanted to be the first customer on her list of buyers to contact.

As he pointed his sedan toward the parking lot of the flea market, he could see most of the vendors packing to leave. It was too hot and too late in the morning for the high-paying customers. He could imagine them hurrying home to air conditioning and iced tea and family time in front of televisions.

Something he'd never experienced before. Not that he would enjoy television anyway.

He'd have to hustle to the back lots where the most interesting vendors displayed their tables of goods. He stretched, reached for his cane and started the trek. He thought about leaving his vest and tweed hat in the car, but he was a gentleman, and that was not possible.

He reached the back of the market to find young Gabe boxing up his wares.

"Anything of interest, my good man?"

"You're late, buddy. Closing shop." Gabe's cheap pop-up tent did little to ward off the rising sun. Noon was an hour away, and the heat was already smothering.

"May I perhaps have a look-see?" Earl persisted.

Gabe shrugged and nodded toward the end of the table. "I've got to get out of this heat, so make it quick."

Gabe's specialty was finding rarities. He had the youthful legs and stamina that the old man no longer possessed. Gabe traveled long distances to auctions and real estate sales, gathering antiques to resell for profit at the market.

Earl pilfered through a half-dozen boxes, careful not to upset Gabe's packing.

An old rotary phone that was here last time. *Not old enough.*

Early inkwells and fountain pens. *Not interested.*

A reproduction of an antique doorbell. *No reproductions.*

Rusty tin boxes of sewing needles and colorful buttons. *Margaret would have liked these…*

He shook off the intrusive memory and moved to the next box. Sweat caused his eyeglasses to slide down his nose. He pushed them up and continued searching. Crinkled newspapers announcing the assassination of Kennedy hid an interesting lump on the table.

Earl moved the papers aside to reveal an antique camera. It was old. Accordion bellows and a glass plate slot dated somewhere around the mid-1800s. His heart skipped a beat.

Oh, please let today be the day.

He turned the camera over, taking care with the wooden case and frail bellows.

And there it was.

The small, engraved bronze square that haunted his every dream.

Earl stumbled against the side of the table, startling Gabe.

"See. Told you it was hot. Better wrap it up, old guy."

Earl forgave Gabe the insensitive remark. "How much?"

"For you, since it's quittin' time… One hundred bucks. Don't know if it can be fixed, and I don't have any of the parts for it. Sparks shot out of the dumb thing last night. Must've had static buildup or something. Didn't know such a thing could happen on something that old. Anyway, I don't have the time to mess around with it."

Earl glanced at Gabe over the rim of his spectacles and smothered a grin. Sparks were good news.

He nodded politely and reached for his billfold. He thumbed through the contents, found the bill, and handed it to Gabe.

Gabe held the bill up to the sunlight. "This real? Don't look real."

"It's an old bill, and it'll spend just fine, young man." Earl remembered the day the bill was gifted to him and squashed yet another intrusive memory. "Printed before you were even a thought on this planet."

Gabe looked at him warily. "Can I have your phone number in case this doesn't pan out?"

Earl sighed and pulled a card from his billfold. For a kid who dealt with antiques, he sure didn't know his Benjamins. "As a matter of fact, if you find anything else with this type of bronze plate, I'd like to know. Where did you stumble onto this camera?"

Gabe studied the old man's number on the card, wrapped the hundred-dollar bill around it, and stuffed it into his jeans pocket. "Don't remember. I've got so much junk, I throw stuff in a corner until sale time. What's so special about the camera? Some sort of family heirloom?" Gabe put the camera into a box for Earl.

"Something like that. You have a good day, now."

Earl scooped up the box under one arm and the cane in the other hand. If he were twenty years younger, he would have skipped back to the car. He struggled to keep a sober face. Smiling like the Cheshire cat at a flea market lets everyone else know you've scored a treasure. It was like playing a game of high-stakes poker, and he wanted to keep his hand to himself.

CHAPTER 3

THE SCREEN DOOR double-bangs shut behind me. The spring hinge rusted through long ago, and no one is bothered enough with the door's racket to fix it. I hear the diesel engine of the bus rev up as it pulls away from the bottom of the lane. My heart sinks a bit as I realize it's the start of another weekend.

There are three types of kids at school: those who go to learn, those who go to cause or catch up on drama, and those who go to avoid home life. I consider myself firmly in that last group. Things are better with Billy gone, but not by much. Too much tension. I plan on calling Hedge later to make plans to be away from here after the chores are done.

I take the stairs two at a time up to my room, throw my tattered backpack on the bed and look out the window. Granddad is outside the barn, tending to the afternoon watering. Nothing but "home-grown 'maters" for the Andrews family.

The fields stretch for miles. Crops of corn and beans broken by the seams of grassy paths. I wonder how many hours I've spent wandering those tracks near the crops.

Maybe I'll skip calling Hedge and sneak out to the fields.

Mom was home from the city and had baked a batch of brownies.

The aroma calls up the stairs to me. I don my overalls and bound down the steps, two at a time, round the tight corner through the living room nearly tripping on the piano bench. I grab a handful of brownies and try to escape out the back door.

"Hi, Mom. How are you? I missed you and I love you so much!" Mom calls sarcastically after me as I try to skip outside, and I'm not fast enough to dodge the interaction.

I spin and give her a quick peck on the cheek. "Love you, Mom." Before I could spin back toward the door, she catches my arm and cups my freckled face in her hands. She kisses me on the head and lets me go.

"It'd be nice to be appreciated. To know that I'm wanted around here." I pretend not to hear that. She cares more about getting back to the city, back to Billy, than being on the farm. Her constant jabs against life here make me squirm.

Granddad rescues me as he stomps into the kitchen and tosses his head toward the back porch.

"Grab a bucket. You're late." Anyone else who heard Granddad's greeting would've thought him rude, but I know better.

I cram another brownie into my mouth. "Hey, Granddad. I thought about going to Hedge's tomorrow. Anything I can do to help before I go?" I know from experience that escaping the tension between my parents and Granddad requires my complete absence from the property —but not before the chores are done. I also know from experience that my parents could care less where I spend my weekends, so long as I wasn't a burden to them. My stomach churns from the combination of scarfing brownies and the anticipation of the answer.

"Spruce up the coop yard and mow the grass around the house. I'll handle the rest."

Wow. That was easy. "You okay, Granddad?"

He finally makes eye contact with me, and his face softens. "Fine. A bit tired today."

"I don't have to go tomorrow. I can stay and help." I don't want to stick around, but something seems off. Especially after all the sappiness from the old guy yesterday.

"No. No. You do what I say then go on. I've got things to do tomorrow that you can't help me with anyway."

I nod and head outside. *Always too young, too scrawny, too...*

The adults always dished out the chores, but never fully trusted me to handle anything beyond chickens for too long. Even Granddad still feels the need to keep me in the dark.

The chickens' water bins are completely dry. The first official day of summer is three weeks away and the heat is already unbearable.

Summer. My stomach churns again. Week after week of parents and stress.

At least summer break will be shorter this year.

I decide to mow first since Dad is about due home. If I'm on the mower, I can delay the father speech for a few minutes, at least. I clear out some clutter from around the front of the riding lawn mower.

The stress was so intense last school year that I'd thought about flunking out of some classes on purpose. I could spend a few hours every day at school through the summer to make up the work. But whenever it was time to turn in an assignment or take an exam, my stomach would scream, and I'd cave under the pressure to continue my Honor Roll streak. Thinking about Granddad's disappointment had a lot to do with me not being able to go through with the plan.

I also didn't want to end up like Billy. He's family, but not really. I should love him. Or at least like him. But I don't. And the mounting tension between the adults ever since we'd moved here often masks the warm, fuzzy vibes one should have for family.

It takes me four tries to get the mower started. After the third try, I realize the tank is out of gas. I'm glad Granddad is preoccupied with other matters, or I would've gotten an earful about the screwup. I gas it up and speed the rider out of the barn, engaging the blades. Stale grass spits from underneath, soon to be replaced with the scent of fresh-cut vegetation. The hum of the engine drowns out all other distractions and allows me to think.

When Granny died, Granddad needed help with the farm because he refused to sell it. "It must stay in the family no matter what." So we moved.

Well, I moved. Mom and Dad split their time between jobs in the city and life here on the weekends.

Mom hates it here. The internet is slow, the TV dish goes out every time the breeze blows, and the floors always need mopped. She cries a lot every weekend.

I whip the mower around the back of the house, spraying grass in the wrong direction. I turn the machine around so the blower faces away from the landscaping and speed up again.

Dad found a new job south of the city, but commuting wasn't cheap. The farmland was worth a small fortune and selling it off would mean we could all move back to Chicago. But Granddad would have none of it. He wouldn't allow anyone but family to tend to the fields, either, other than his old buddies down the road—and all of them suffering from one ailment or another. Bunch of old codgers—even Granddad sometimes.

Dad's blue Intrepid peels into the drive, throwing gravel into the yard. I'd have to be careful not to throw rocks with the mower. He waves at me and I wave back. Maybe Dad was in a better mood this weekend than last. I spin the mower toward the house in time to see Dad pause on the porch. His chest swells up. He slowly exhales and hangs his head before opening the door.

So maybe not better than last weekend.

I would prefer to stay outside—either on the mower or in the fields —than to be caged inside with Mom and Dad.

Or in front of a screen like Hedge.

Hedge and I've been friends since my family moved to the area. He was one of those kids who went to school to learn. Goodness only knows why; Hedge was smarter than most of the teachers in our small-town school. Hedge has been odd-man-out most of his life, so we get along fine. I don't care to know anyone else and I don't mind Hedge's quirks, so it works out.

Opposites attract, I suppose.

It takes me a couple of hours to finish the yard. I stomp off the grass from my pant legs and round the back into the kitchen. Mom and

Dad are in the living room, arguing. Nothing new, and no better than last weekend.

I need to stop my wishful thinking; it only gives me emotional whiplash.

I stop at the back wall of the kitchen, listening. My heart pounds in my chest and I think I might throw up. Their fights become louder and longer with each passing month.

"I can't take it anymore, Jim."

"Just a few more weeks, and we'll be done."

"No, I mean you. I can't wait for you. You keep saying we'll leave, but we never do."

"For heaven's sake, Marie, you're only here on the weekends! What's the matter with you?" Dad whispers some more stuff that I can't quite catch.

"Jim, I want a divorce." Mom hurries into the kitchen, startles and pauses briefly when she sees me and realizes I'd heard what she'd said. Tears flow down her cheeks, and she bounds out the back door.

Dad follows close behind, also startled to see me. My eyes feel stuck open wide and all the blood in my face has drained to my ankles. "It'll be alright. We'll figure this out, Buddy." He tousles my hair, still caked with grass and sweat, and heads after his wife.

I slide to the floor. Not feeling. Not thinking.

The walls begin to close around me, and the black hole of a crippled family attempts to swallow me entirely.

Until the deafening shotgun blast hurls me back into this pathetic moment.

CHAPTER 4

I STAND on shaking legs to peek out the back door.

"Get in the house. Now." Granddad waves his hunting gun at Mom and Dad who stand in the driveway like pale wax mannequins, stuck in shocked awe. Granddad pumps the gun and points it toward the sky. "Don't make me fire off another one. I said *house*. Now."

That works and Mom and Dad back stumble toward the porch and up the steps into the coat room off the kitchen, Granddad close behind. As Mom makes her way to the living room, Granddad carefully unloads the shotgun and sets it in the corner. Dad stands trembling next to me.

I find my voice. "Granddad, what's going on?"

"I know exactly what I'm doing. Your parents are going to ruin everything." Granddad points to the living room. "Get in there with your wife, Jim. Oliver, up to your room. Now."

Dad puts a hand on my shoulder. "Go on, get upstairs and lock the bedroom door." I pull away to obey Dad's command, but not before he slips a cell phone into my overalls pocket. In a barely audible whisper he says, "9-1-1."

"I heard that. Give me the phone, Oliver. And go to your room. Stay there until I call you."

I'm frozen once again. I don't know who to listen to, and I dare not move as I gaze at the gun propped in the corner. Too much has happened in the last ninety seconds to process.

Divorce.

Gunfire.

9-1-1.

Granddad's gone nuts…

The old man reaches into my pocket and pulls out the phone. He goes to the back door and tosses it far into the yard. He gives me a gentle shove toward the stairs. "Get going."

My feet feel as though they are cast in concrete blocks. I go, but I weigh a thousand pounds. I reach the doorway to my room and slam the door, but I remain in the hallway so I can listen.

"…not going to say this more than once," Granddad is saying. His voice is controlled, but I can sense great tension underneath. Like the time when he kicked Billy out. "I've tried to explain how I want you to take care of the farm. It's not an option. It's not a choice. It's life and death, and you must do it, Jim. Your mother would have wanted it this way." Granddad's voice shakes at the mention of Granny.

"Marie and I don't want to farm, Dad. We've *never* wanted that. I can't find a good job around here. Marie's miserable and ready to leave me over this dumb place. What's so important about this piece-of-junk property in the middle of nowhere?" Dad's voice is not so controlled.

I hear Mom sobbing in the corner, mumbling something about Billy and wanting to leave. My heart beats in my ears. I wrap my arms around my middle and will the churning to stop.

"It's not about a profession. Get any crazy job you want, but you must see to the property!" The wooden planks of the living room floor creak under what must be Granddad's work boots pacing back and forth. "Look. I can't get into it all right now, but I'll call the other farm owners tonight to set up an emergency meeting. You *will* be there. Both of you. You must understand I'm not simply a washed-up farmer who wants his land to remain in his family. Please hang on until tomorrow when we can all meet. Marie. You can hold off calling a divorce attorney for that long, right?"

"Already called him."

"What?" Dad screams. "We didn't discuss anything, for crying out loud. I'm doing the best—"

"Enough!" Granddad shouts. "Marry. Separate. Divorce. Whatever. The land stays with the Andrews men. Maybe it's best if Marie heads up to the city tonight, Jim. You, me, and the other farmers'll sort this out tomorrow."

"No, Dad. My wife just told me she's filed for divorce. And you're worried about piles of dirt." There's a scuffle then Dad shouts again. "Marie, wait!"

The front screen door slams and have to go into my room to see out over the driveway. Mom and Dad are arguing at her car. She is already in the driver's seat with the ignition running. I can't hear them without opening the window. Mom starts backing up the car, and Dad jogs alongside as she drives backward out of sight, leaving Dad alone in the middle of the gravel drive.

This is like one of Hedge's dumb reality video games where you lose control of all your SIMS and they begin to have a mind of their own.

Not that I ever had control to begin with.

After many miserable minutes, Dad comes into the house and I move back to the hall.

"I hope you're happy, old man. Your temper tantrum cost me my marriage!"

"That marriage was doomed before it started, and you know it. Hey, where are you going?"

"Chicago. I've got to straighten this out."

Granddad booms, "You're not listening! You have no idea what's at stake—"

"I don't give a rip, Dad. Do whatever. I'm done discussing this. The way you're going on, it would seem you're into something illegal. Drugs? Slave labor, maybe? I'm getting Oliver and we're leaving."

Granddad pleads now. "No, Jim. Please don't take him. Please don't put him in the middle of the mess with you and Marie. Let him stay here."

"With you? You're likely to shoot him if his mower lines aren't perfectly parallel!" Dad stomps up the stairs and I scurry to the bed as Dad bursts into the doorway.

"Pack. We're leaving."

"No. What about school? What about Hedge? No." I try to be forceful, but the energy transfers into tears on the last few words until I sob. "How could you let Mom leave like that? How could you take me away from here?"

Dad sits down next to me and starts rubbing my back, but I pull away. "I don't care if he's crazy. I want to stay."

Dad's shoulders slump and he puts his head in his hands. "I didn't plan any of this, Son. I don't know what to do."

I see an opening. I wipe a string of tears and snot onto my sleeve and sit up straight. "Just let me finish school. You and Mom sort things out. I know you will. I've been okay here with Granddad all week long while you and Mom work. Leave me here. I'll be one less worry." I'd always figured my parents only worried about me superficially anyway. I'm their duty. A burden for them to spend money on and occasionally throw some time at, but I'm not their top priority.

"It would be irresponsible of me to leave you here." Dad nods toward the stairs. "With him."

"That's what I'm trying to say, Dad. I've been with him alone. For months. He's never acted like this. He really loves it here. I love it here. I think he's afraid to be alone."

Dad sits quietly for a few minutes then takes a deep breath and straightens. "I need to sort things out with your mom."

"Leave me. I'll finish school strong. I'll make you proud. I'll look after Granddad and you get Mom back." I don't believe that last bit. About getting Mom back. I'm not sure Dad could ever get her back.

Dad puts a trembling arm around me and gives me a half-hearted hug. "You're stronger than you know, Son. I am proud of you."

"Thanks. I'll be okay." I feel Dad starting to cave to my request.

"Okay. I want a phone call every day. Every. Day. And if he does that again, or if you think something illegal or unethical is going on here, I want to know right away, and you'll come with me. No arguments. Understand?"

"Yes. I don't have a phone." The landline doesn't work if it's rainy or windy. Cell service is spotty, but you could usually get a bar or two outside or upstairs. Dad pulls cash out of his pocket, probably all he had on him, and hands it to me.

"Mom said you were going to Hedge's tomorrow. Stop at the drugstore and pick up a cell phone. Call me right away with your number. Call your mom, too. I know she'll want to hear from you."

I nod and put the cash in the dresser drawer. Dad stands. We embrace again, and Dad goes to pack.

I watch from my window as a fragile relief settles over me, even though I know the grieving is about to start. Granddad was probably right. Mom and Dad were never good matches for one another, but they are my parents. Even with all their fights and turmoil, I can't imagine them not together.

Dad makes his way outside with his duffle. Most of his belongings are still in the city for the work week. He has words with Granddad again, fishes his cell from the yard, and leaves in his car. Just like Mom.

Granddad sits in his old pickup truck, holding something small and black next to his ear. I never knew Granddad owned a phone other than the corded one in the kitchen.

He leaves the truck, stares out to the east field, rubs his hand across his stressed, wrinkled face and walks toward the house.

I'm not sure whether to run down to meet him or stay upstairs, but I venture to the kitchen—if for no other reason than it's closer to the bathroom. The nausea is settling in hard.

Granddad slumps at the kitchen table. He always takes the seat that faces the fields. He glances up at me and rests his head in his hands.

"Sorry you had to witness all of that. It wasn't my intention to scare you or harm them. They just won't listen."

"That's okay." I hold my arms crossed over my gut and lean against the counter. I have no idea what to say or do next.

"Your dad said you can stay until the end of summer. By then he and Marie should have things settled one way or another."

"Okay."

Granddad takes a deep breath. "You go on with Hedge tomorrow. Like you planned. Don't worry 'bout nothing in the morning but the chickens. I'll give you a ride into town."

"Okay." I decide it best not to add comments or ask questions. I go out the back door to tend to the nightly watering, glad to be out of the house. The evening is cooling from the blistering heat earlier. The chickens are happy to see me, or at least as happy as chickens could be. My whole world was about to change.

And probably not for the best.

I fight back tears as I toss the water bucket into the corner of the barn. I see flashes in the distance. Probably heat lightning, but it looks green.

Even the weather seems to be under the stress of the universe.

CHAPTER 5

I AM in no way recovered from the stress of Friday night. I slide out of bed and dress for the trip to town with Granddad. I stuff the cash Dad gave me into my jeans and grab my backpack. May as well try to study for the math test while Hedge dives deep into the world of SIMS.

My stomach growls, and as I reach the aroma-filled kitchen, I realize that no one had eaten dinner last night. The last food I had was that handful of brownies, and those I'd lost in the middle of the night—along with the school's ever-popular Friday cardboard pizza lunch.

Granddad sits at the table in front of an almost-empty plate. Bacon and eggs steam from my plate. He nods for me to sit with him.

"You okay, Son?" He folds his newspaper into his lap and meets my eyes.

No. I'm not at all okay. I muster courage to ask Granddad the question that had pressed on my chest all night. "You wouldn't hurt them, would you?" Tears fall from my eyes without my permission. I especially hate tears in front of Granddad who already thinks I can't handle even the smallest stressors.

"No, Son. Not at all. I just—I needed them to understand how important this place is." Now Granddad tears up. I slide into my chair.

His tears make mine fall faster, and a few splash onto my scrambled eggs.

"Why, though? And they left anyway."

Granddad stands and takes his plate to the sink. "It's nothing for you to worry about today. I know you're upset, but try to eat." He puts his heavy hands on my shoulders. "Maybe you should pack a bag to stay the weekend with Hedge. I'll clear it with his mom. Give this situation some time to cool down and for me to talk some sense into your dad." I glance toward the corner at the shotgun, and Granddad leans in close. "I promise it will stay in the corner." He squeezes my shoulders tight and heads out the back door.

I finish as much breakfast as I can, scrape my plate and go pack for Hedge's. I try to imagine Hedge's reaction when I tell him about the events that had unfolded. I imagine his jaw-drop, wide-eyed gaze and his hand paused midair above the Cheetos bag as he takes in my story.

I open the window to my bedroom and let the fresh morning breeze whisk away the staleness of the long night. I hear Granddad talking to our neighbor Eddie. Their voices trail up the side of the house and tumble muffled into the room with me—some words I can make out, others not. The old men stand in the dusty lane, both in overalls. They should be on one of those Future Farmers of America posters. *This could be you...*

Eddie is older than Granddad, and meaner, too. The last time I saw Eddie was when another old farmer died of cancer a few months back and Granddad made everyone accompany him to the funeral home. That was the second time I'd ever seen Granddad wear anything other than overalls. The other time he was in a suit was at Granny's funeral.

The men continue to talk about the meeting with the other landowners to happen in the morning. My family is in turmoil and Granddad's still pounding on about the farm. It doesn't make sense. The farm isn't going anywhere. The family, though...

I try to stifle the what-if's and finish stuffing clothes and the rest of my homework into the backpack. Halfway down the stairs I realize I forgot my toothbrush, but I don't care. It was Hedge, after all, and Granddad is hollering for me to get in the truck.

Eddie pulls away as I climb into the old pickup. It smells of sweat and gasoline. The driver's seat belt had stopped latching years ago. Granddad wasn't worried about the seat belt and said if it was his time to go, it was his time to go. He'd said that he'd get it fixed before I was old enough to drive. "Gotta make a stop before Hedge's house."

We barrel down the drive, and I tighten my grip on the door's arm rest. I always feel like I'm gambling with death when Granddad is on a mission. Sometimes I see my pathetic life flash before my eyes when he takes the S-curve near the ravine. With Granddad behind the wheel, the normal ten-minute drive to Fallston only takes five.

I think his lifetime goal is to shave it down to three.

We pull into the police station's lot—a tiny, four-parking-spot slab of asphalt, and two spots are taken up by the town's only two police cars. I sit dizzy from the drive and stunned at our location as Granddad shuts off the engine. "What are we doing here?"

"I'll only be a minute." He slides out of the truck and meets the chief at the door. I can't hear what they say, but the old chief hands Granddad a folder with Fallston's bold and glorious town seal on the cover.

The small town has this tiny police station, a handful of restaurants —mostly locally owned diners that serve the widower farmers a couple meals a day—the school, library, and, surprisingly, a small hospital. No one quite understands how a town this size sustains its very own ER, but an aging population probably has something to do with it. The joke among the locals is the hospital would go out of business if the farmers ever stopped slicing open their hands on their rusty old equipment—or if the cure to pneumonia is found. We also have a one-screen theater that never shows anything rated over PG, and the movies they do run stay in town for weeks at a time. About ten movies a year is all we get.

I try to calm my breathing. I roll down my window, expecting the same breeze from earlier, but stale humidity has taken its place. I stare at the white cinderblocks of the station's walls and wonder how busy anyone inside could be. The running theory is that the Fallston police only serve the farmers' calls of vandalism or trespassing. All other complaints go unattended.

Granddad gets back in and tosses an envelope between us. I reach for it, but Granddad snatches it away and moves it under his seat, but not before I spot Mom's name on the front. He turns to me. "Nothing for you to worry about, Oliver."

"Did Mom turn you in? Are we in more trouble?" My stomach scrambles my eggs for the second time.

"No. Andy handled it. No problems. And nothing for you to worry about."

Yeah, nothing for me *to worry about.* I remember the cash for the phone and desperately want to call Dad. To ask him if he'd found Mom and if they were patching things up.

And to ask if she turned Granddad in.

We pull in front of Hedge's house a minute later. "Take care. I'll pick you up tomorrow evening. Stay out of trouble, now." Granddad pats me on the back. I manage a smile and jump from the truck. I stand in Hedge's yard and watch as Granddad speeds out of sight.

Dumped. Like a little kid.

Hedge bounds out of the house, nearly knocking me to the ground with a from-the-behind chest bump. It takes him a moment to realize that I'm not quite right.

"Hey, you look awful, man." Hedge is a bit on the pudgy side and always a bit unkempt. He wears the same T-shirt for days in a row. When puberty hit, his mom insisted he wash his clothes more often. At my insistence, Hedge has at least started wearing deodorant.

"Thanks, Hedge. Had a bad day yesterday."

"What's going on?" Hedge grabs my pack and bounces it in his hand, testing out the weight. "I thought you were only coming for the afternoon."

"Mom wants a divorce. I gotta buy a phone. Dad left her. Granddad pulled a gun on them yesterday."

Hedge looked at me, speechless for only a moment. "Tough break, man." We walk toward the house. "Video games, pizza, and solve the world's problems?"

"I'll skip the pizza, but the rest sounds good." I tell Hedge about the events in detail, trying not to sob. Hedge plays his video game the whole time, but that's Hedge. That's how he processes.

"Well, I can solve one of those problems right now." He tosses the controller to the couch and leaves the room. When he comes back, he's holding an old flip-phone. His first one from a year ago. "Still works. We keep it around just in case. Still has minutes on it, too. Enough to call your dad a few times." He flings it at my head.

I duck and have to reach behind the couch to retrieve the phone. "Wow. Thanks."

"Now, I can solve another one of your problems, too."

"How so?"

"We need pizza and a plan."

"It's still morning—"

"Pizza," Hedge holds a finger at my face. "Then a plan." Hedge leaves for the kitchen. He does his best thinking playing video games. He does his hyper-drive thinking with video games and pizza sauce dripping down his chin. "Pepperoni or supreme?"

"Neither. You go ahead."

"Suit yourself." As Hedge fires up the oven, I make my way to the front porch with the phone. Hedge's street is quaint and quiet. Each house a cookie-cutter replica of the next. Nice and predictable. I turn the phone over in my hand and remember Dad's face when he handed me the cash. There's nothing cookie-cutter about my current ordeal.

I dial Dad's number, but only get a voicemail. I hang up without saying anything, but I change my mind and redial. "Hey, Dad. I'm at Hedge's for the weekend. The number on your caller ID is the new phone number. Hope you and Mom are working things out." My voice is about to crack, so I hang up. I'm sick to death of my mouse voice and watering eyes.

I dial Mom next, but her voicemail is full. Probably a hundred of her closest city friends wishing her the best. And none of them left room for her son…

"Get in here. Don't you want to hear my plan? We've got eighteen minutes before the pizza's done."

It's only ten a.m. I can't imagine how many more pizzas it will take to get through the weekend. "Coming."

Hedge flops onto the floor and resumes his game. "You know what else we need?"

"If you say Oreos, I'm gonna smack you in the face."

Hedge grins. "We need a map. You know, like the one the kid in *Home Alone* used to take down the robbers."

"I don't think that applies in this situation. We're not being robbed." I slump to the floor.

"No foolin'. Hear me out."

"Okay. I'm listening, oh great and powerful Brain. Tell thy humble servant thy plan to solve divorce, gun battles, and a land dispute."

"We need to go to that meeting tomorrow morning."

I sit up straight. "If Granddad catches us, we'll—"

"Yeah, yeah. He'll shoot me in the kneecap and you in the rear end. Really? What's he gonna do? And besides, we won't get caught. We just gotta be *careful*." I stare at the screen as Hedge defeats the dragon. His avatar stands on top of the dragon and air-pumps his flaming sword. Hedge raises his arms above his head in victory. His deodorant is fading, but I don't care.

I ponder Hedge's plan and mumble, "We just gotta be careful."

The oven timer dings, and I feel hunger for the first time since stepping off the bus yesterday.

CHAPTER 6

"WE DON'T KNOW when this meeting will happen," I complain. Timing is the biggest issue with our grand scheme.

"If that's the only plot hole we've got, Hollywood should hire us as writers. Have you *seen* the last couple of movies? What messes!"

I haven't seen a movie in ages, but if Hedge says they have plot issues, then they have plot issues.

We'd planned and brainstormed every possible outcome for most of Saturday afternoon and late into the night. None of it made any real sense—our plan or what this meeting was all about, and we could only hope we had it figured out as best we could.

We gather supplies—some water bottles, Oreos, and a flashlight as an afterthought—and head on foot toward the farm before dawn Sunday morning.

We try to be quiet as we cross the small patch of trees and the creek at the bottom of Granddad's lane. We'd planned to wait there, hidden in the tree line, until the old man went out to feed the chickens, then we'd sneak into the basement and camp out under the air vents where you could hear voices floating down the stairwell near the washer and dryer.

As if on cue, Granddad comes out the front. The screen door slams loudly behind him, and he disappears around the corner of the house. I wince. We'd have to remember to hold the screen until it was all the way closed or we'd be caught before we ever reach the basement, for sure. "We gotta move now. It doesn't take that long to feed chickens."

Hedge nods. We grab our packs and race across the front yard. We reach the edge of the porch and carefully slide off our boots, dusty and with a layer of mud from the walk here and crossing the creek. We take the boots with as we cross the porch and grab the screen door. We hear gravel spraying from under tires at the end of the lane.

"Hurry!"

Hedge nearly pushes me into the living room. "Who's that coming already? Isn't it too early?" He ran out of breath halfway to the farm, and now sweat falls from every pore in his body. I hope whoever it is won't be able to smell Hedge's trail lingering in the living room.

We make it through the kitchen and to the basement door as voices start up outside. We scale down the steps and let out synchronized sighs of relief. "Your shoes didn't drip mud, did they?" Crossing the creek was the only way not to be seen sneaking onto the property.

"Stop stewing, Oliver. I didn't have time to check, and it's too late now. I hear someone in the kitchen." We stop our hurried whispers to listen. I recognize the voice arguing with Granddad.

"Dad!" I jump. My legs start for the stairs with a mind of their own and without my permission. Hedge grabs me by the back of the shirt.

"Stick to the mission, stupid." Hedge glares, and I know he's right. There is no way we're getting out of the basement until after the meeting—and the plan for getting out is shakier than the plan for getting in. My gut rumbles loudly.

"Shut that thing up and get a grip!" Hedge hands me a water bottle.

"Can't help it. I'm gonna puke." I use the bottle on my forehead, replacing my sweat with the bottle's condensation.

"Oh, no. Not down here. Not next to me. You'll get me goin' and then it'll be a sewage fest. Drink. Maybe that will help."

I take a sip and breathe deeply. Fabric softener mingled with must hangs in the air around us, but the water trickling down my esophagus settles me a bit. I find a wooden crate and position it under the open vent. Hedge does the same with an upside-down five-gallon bucket. "*You* should sit on the bucket. You know. In case."

I throw my bottle cap at Hedge's face and take another sip of the tepid water. Hedge grins. "Great plan! Better than a video game! Now we just have to wait. Too bad there's no TV down here."

I slouch on the crate and hold the water bottle to my forehead.

We've been in the musty basement for hours. Every time the AC unit kicks on, we jump. Light barely reaches the floor of the basement through the narrowest of windows that dot the top edge of the wall near the ceiling—windows that haven't been cleaned for years. I refuse to turn on the overhead light for fear we'd be caught if someone cared to open the basement door.

Occasionally, footsteps thud overhead, and the raised tension of voices sneaks its way through the creaky farmhouse floorboards. Nothing is discernable. I think I hear Mom's name a few times, but I can't be sure. I'm sleep-deprived and I want news so badly, I could be fooling myself.

About ten o'clock, we finally hear the rumble of a truck on the drive. Then another.

"Wish we could see what's going on. It sounds like the party's about to start." Hedge tries to position himself closer to the vent.

I dig in the backpack and pull out a notebook and pen. Hedge rolls his eyes. "We're not having an exam over the material, nerd. Just listen!"

"Fine. But one of these days, attention to detail may just save your life. Or at least get you better grades." Hedge rolls his eyes and I lay the notebook aside as the shuffle of feet directly overhead signals the start of the meeting.

"Thanks for coming on short notice." Granddad's voice booms through the vent and we nearly topple off our perches. He must be standing directly over our heads.

A few mumbled greetings, and then Granddad continues. "You

both know my son, of course. His wife, Marie, couldn't be with us today. That's something we'll have to deal with later."

Hedge nudges closer to me. "What does that mean, 'deal with it later?' What's he gonna do?"

I send an elbow to Hedge's gut to shut him up and put some distance between my nose and Hedge's aroma. Hedge clasps his hand over his mouth to stifle a yelp and gives me a dirty look as he retreats to his bucket.

"—don't understand why you're doing this. Just let us be, Dad. Let my wife and I work out our lives without interference from half the county. You do know Marie called the police."

Eddie's voice is next. The farmer from the driveway yesterday. "What your estranged wife doesn't understand is how the police in this town operate. We do our own policing. Us three. Well, it used to be us four until the cancer got Frank and he, well—"

"What Eddie means is we run the police department with people we have chosen. I know she filed a complaint. The report is under the seat of my truck. You can call them, too, if you want. But since domestic disputes are handled at the local level, going further up the chain won't do you any good. Calm down, Jim. Hear us out." Granddad sounds aggravated as more feet shuffle overhead. He continues. "Marie is a problem for another day. We're here to discuss the land. The deed needs to be passed on soon. None of us are getting any younger."

"I don't want this land. I want my life back. And I don't care about *their* farms, either." I imagine Dad pointing angrily at the other men in the room.

The deepest voice of all speaks. "This land holds a secret that must be kept at all costs. We came today to help your father explain, as best we can, why this property must be protected. And why no one, *ever*, can know what's on it."

This time Hedge elbows my gut. "They have to know we're down here listening, and they're yanking our chains. This is crap! No one talks like this."

"Shut up, moron. Listen." I stand so my ear is closer to the vent.

Dad starts to protest, but the deep-voiced farmer interrupts him. I can't remember the name or the face that belongs to this graveled voice.

"A couple hundred years ago, these acres were all part of a small town, not farmland. And over the horizon line there," again, I imagine the old guy pointing and I wish I could see which direction, "stood an elegant lamppost at an intersection of a couple of cobblestone roads. Our families' ancestors lived on the corners: Frank's folks, Eddie's folks, my folks and the Andrews gang. Terrible things happened under that light. Things that have haunted all four families since that time."

"Meeting's over." Dad must have jumped to his feet because I hear chair legs scoot across the hardwood floor. "Some light some hundred years ago and what? What now? My dad held my wife and I at *gunpoint* yesterday and demanded I join this circus. You're all nuts."

I glance at Hedge who nods in agreement and motions "crazy" with his finger near his head, but his eyes are glued to the vent. "We've now entered the Twilight Zone." I answer him with a punch to the leg.

The farmer continues. "Once in a while, a great flash of sparks would fly from that dang pole and, well. How'd you put it? Anyone nearby would be well, how'd you say—"

The air conditioner kicks on. We jump, knocking over the crate I'd been sitting on. We freeze, hoping we haven't been exposed, but the blower to the AC unit must have masked the clanging.

I panic. "I can't hear them over the AC. We've got to get out of here now before we get caught. I think we've heard too much."

"Agreed. This is too much. Sounds like they're still in the living room. Out the back!" Hedge starts for the staircase. "Shoes. Grab the shoes!"

I gather our mud-caked boots and follow Hedge up the basement steps to the kitchen. As we open the back screen, we hear the argument heating up in the living room. We sneak onto the back porch, down the side of the yard and back to the tree line. We are all the way to the creek before we dare stop to put our shoes on.

"Dumb central air."

"Yeah. Middle-class sucks, doesn't it?" I roll my eyes.

"Whatcha gonna do now? That didn't solve anything. What light post? I've never seen some old light pole anywhere around here."

"He said it was at the corner of the properties when the area used to be a town. Someone had to have bulldozed the buildings and let things grow up. The light may not be there anymore." I look toward the east where the properties meet.

The east where I've never been—not so far as I can remember.

"I say we find the pole and get some answers. Take a shovel. We could find some old coins or something cool like that. This is way better than video games." Hedge wipes sweat from his face on the tail of his shirt, now muddy from carrying his boots. He digs in the bag, holds out some Oreos for me, smiling as he takes a bite. He has black goo caking in his teeth that complements the mud all over his face.

I stare at him for a second. "This is why you will never have a girlfriend."

"I don't need some high-maintenance woman." Hedge grins at me again. "I've got you."

We walk back to town to clean up before Granddad comes for me. We decide to meet later for a "hike" if anyone were to care enough to ask. I know Hedge won't blow my secret. I can always count on Hedge.

What I can't count on any longer is wishful thinking for a peaceful home—not even the *illusion* of one, for that matter. "Someday" is never going to come for the Andrews family.

Mom, Dad, Granddad and this circus, as Dad had called it, has changed everything.

I think about what will happen if Mom and Dad do make things right and we move back to Chicago. Near Billy. Away from Granddad and the farm. Despite the heat, goosebumps rise from the nape of my neck and ripple down to my wrists.

I can't let this happen.

CHAPTER 7

HEDGE and I pause at the tree line down from my gravel drive. We don backpacks and the same muddy boots from earlier today.

Dad had finally called me as we were walking back to town. He sounded shook up and said he was still in Chicago. Yet another lie to keep me in the dark and yet another reason for my stomach to wrench again. Stomach issues were the only constant in this mess.

Granddad had called Hedge's mom earlier to see if I could stay over one more night and ride to school with Hedge Monday morning. He'd bring me appropriate clothes later Sunday night. That was fine with her and it left us more time to explore and figure out what the old cronies had been talking about in the meeting.

"Any idea which direction?" Hedge scopes the edge of the Andrews' land and I pull out a crumpled line map that I'd scribbled while Hedge had reloaded on pizza. Hedge had gotten more exercise in the last twelve hours than in the last twelve weeks.

"Granddad never let me go to the east field. I think we start there."

Hedge grabs the map and presses it against my back. He picks up a muddy stick and marks a solid X on the east field. "And right here, here is where we'll find the mystery of all mysteries. Maybe gold. Maybe diamonds or maybe, maybe a dead body—"

"You're a moron." I stuff the map into the backpack and try to wipe the dirt off my back. I don't want to think about what we might find. Not really. Not after the escapade with the gun a couple days before. What if Granddad was in some kind of trouble? What if there was nowhere to go for help because the police were in on it?

Whatever *it* is.

I try to think of anything else. But everything else was stressful, too. "Dad lied to me. I think he and Mom are gonna split this time."

"Sorry 'bout that, man. I know it's rough. Glad my dad took off before I could understand what I was missing from an intact family." Hedge's dad had left when Hedge was in elementary school. His mom worked all the time, and Hedge has no siblings. I don't have any, either, unless you count Billy.

But I stopped counting Billy a long time ago.

We walk the grassy lane as far as we can before it ends in rows of corn as high as our heads. Barely three rows in, the long, thin leaves of the corn cut my exposed skin. "Should've worn long sleeves," I say as I shield my face from the stalks. Five rows in, Hedge fell victim, as well.

"Too dang hot for long sleeves. We'll wipe the blood up later." Hedge drips sweat for the second time today. "I'd rather bleed out than die of heat stroke."

We slow our pace to retrieve water bottles from the packs. "How far do you think we've walked?" Hedge downs half the bottle then pours the rest over his head.

"Probably not as far as it feels, especially with all the complaining you're doing. Give me a boost."

Hedge moans and kneels between the corn. He cups his hands out, braced by his knee, and lets me stand with one foot in his hands to get a view over the corn.

"I see a clearing. Maybe another irrigation lane." Hedge wobbles, and I topple between the sharp blades, gaining a slice on the cheek for my efforts. "Nice! Not sure how I'll explain this." I try to wipe the blood pouring from the cut.

"Sorry man. For a scrawny kid, you weigh more than I expected."

Hedge brushes off the dirt and helps me up. "You wanna wipe on my shirt?"

"I'll pass. Let's keep moving." My face stings and my feet hurt. The blistering hot weather doesn't aid morale, but I have to know what is out here. Actually, I want to get the whole thing over with. Hedge probably feels like he's in a reality video game. I'm weary of the tension and fighting. Reality—*real* reality—sucks.

"Hey, those fields would've been easier to walk through." Hedge points east as we approach the clearing—a clearing which is not a tractor path or irrigation lane at all. I stop and stare.

It isn't a meadow or an unplanted swatch of ground, either. Irrigation lanes, fences, trees, or a creek should have marked the edges of the fields, no matter who owned them. Granddad had planted the corn, which we'd trudged through. Corn grows in the adjacent area, probably the land Granddad bought from Frank's kids after Frank died. Wheat and soybeans grow in the other fields owned by Eddie and the deep-voiced guy.

"Those fields have to be owned by the other men. Granddad never planted wheat this year. He said it wasn't worth the hassle this spring."

The clearing we stand in is at least thirty yards in all directions from the edge of the crops. In dead center stands a tall, thin metallic pole with some apparatus on the top. "Like they described," I point at the pole. Hedge gasps for air, partly from the physical exertion and, by the look in his eyes, partly from the excitement of the hunt.

The ground is not soil or sod in the odd clearing. Instead, broken bricks with bits of grass peeking through carpet the area. But even the grass stops growing a few feet away from the crops. The closer you get to the pole, there is nothing but brick.

Hedge points in all directions. "You can see where there'd have been streets, now all busted to pieces. Who keeps this up? Who comes all the way out here to spray for weeds and keep the grass down?" Hedge kicks at some of the brick bits, but they don't move. "Huh."

Hedge is fully invested in the mystery despite the bloody cuts and sweltering heat.

I have more questions than answers. Actually, I have no answers at all. I had almost believed Hedge in the basement this morning about the whole story being made up to trick us somehow. That all the men standing above our heads had found out we were eavesdropping and were being cruel, telling tall tales to teach us a lesson.

I bend to pick up a faded brick piece, but it doesn't budge, as if it is cemented in place. I nod toward the pole. "Let's check it out."

As we approach the center of the clearing and near the pole, we can make out the details on the antique post. This is nothing like the aluminum lampposts in town. This one is amazingly detailed. The light is attached directly on top of the post and multiple glass panels angle around the element inside. Along the pole are intricate carvings of square-toothed gears and gadgets like from the inside of a clock. Raised iron vines wrap from the base all the way to the top. Occasionally, a rose or daisy etching peeks from behind a cogwheel. The artwork travels from the base of the pole, gears toppling, and vines etched in time, all the way to the casing of the light.

At one point, I think I see the gears spin and the vines twist and snake. I pull back for a second to rub my eyes. Has to be lack of sleep and the heat playing tricks.

Neither of us have taken our eyes off the pole, and we circle it a dozen times. Hedge breaks the silent dance without breaking his gaze on the pole. "Wouldn't something as old as this be covered in rust and holes, or even a few gunshots from masked bank robbers back in the day, or something?"

He was referring to the Fallston Gang who, years ago, had shot up the streets, signs, and barns. They attempted to rob the bank after a bad batch of moonshine stole their good sensibilities. I'd always imagined Billy was related to one of those gang members whenever I'd heard the tales in school or from Granddad.

"You'd think," I agree. The metal has held my gaze captive since I entered the clearing. "Actually, it shouldn't be here at all." I reach out to touch the pole, the mysterious scroll-worked iron beckoning me, but Hedge pulls my arm away.

"What are you doing? Don't touch it!"

"Why not? It's just a post." I finally pull my eyes out of their trance to focus on Hedge, who is dead serious for the first time in a long while. "Okay. I won't. Yet."

I circle the post again when something at the base draws my attention. Brick and pebbles partially obscure it, but I can make out the edge of some sort of a plate. I reach out again.

"I said don't touch it." Hedge bumps me hard with his knee.

"What's got you so spooked? I'm just gonna try to move the rocks and see what this is—"

I try to move the obscuring pieces, but like the rest of the broken street all around us, they won't budge. Lying down on my stomach, eye-level with the base of the pole, I can make out lettering, but I can't read it. It's the only time-worn thing on the whole post.

Hedge taps me with the toe of his boot. "Do you hear that?" He tilts his ear close to the post and I raise to join him, both of us careful not to touch the pole.

A hum, something like an electric vibration, has started at the base of the pole.

"Did you touch something down there?"

"No, I swear on my Granny's grave!" I look back to the plaque. I had only touched the gravel. I'm sure of it.

The humming intensifies and travels up the post. The iron scroll-work, gears, and vines wiggle upward with the vibrations, but that's impossible, isn't it?

"Time to go!" I yell and start running toward the safety of the corn rows. Hedge, slower and already worn out, pauses a bit longer.

As he turns to run, the vibration elevates to a high-pitched squeal as sparks fly from the base of the post. The hum turns into a metal-on-metal grinding shriek. About five feet from the base, Hedge is five feet from the post when he looks over his shoulder.

Just as the single light fixture atop the pole flashes green.

Then everything falls silent.

CHAPTER 8

EARL'S HOUSE creaked in the same places he did, groaned as loudly as he did with the changes in weather, and carried the same musty tobacco scent as his clothes and beard. He shut the heavy oak door on the quaint Chicago neighborhood and opened the windows to the parlor. He'd sat the camera on the table the day he bought it from Gabe. He'd glance at it as he passed by on his way to the kitchen for a snack or to go down the hall for the mail drop. He liked the look of it on his table.

The same table he'd hoped to share with Margaret.

He approached the camera, one hand on his aching hip, the other on the knob of his old cane. Today was the day. He couldn't wait any longer.

He turned the camera over and inspected the brass plate. The engraving was barely readable. The camera was from the early 1850s, and this one held a secret. Most people thought the plate worthless—he'd even read some reports of antique collectors trying to dismantle the plates and restore whatever items they'd found to their original condition, only to be surprised when the plates proved impossible to remove. But, the collectors were mostly right. The plates themselves were worthless. There was no value in the brass engraving. The value was what the engraving indicated was *inside* the object.

Or, in this case, inside Earl's camera.

He gently pulled the camera fully open like an accordion. The burgundy bellows needed repair; several moth-eaten spots were evident. The previous owner had no idea what they had possessed. And neither had Gabe.

The glass developing plate was intact, which was a feat in itself. Earl had collected a few such plates and stored them carefully in his cedar trunk. Well, Margaret's cedar trunk. These camera pieces were incredibly fragile and extremely difficult to find.

The camera was missing a few bits here and there, but nothing that Earl hadn't collected over the years. The lens and cap were intact and seemed to be in working order. He retrieved the glass plate holder and chemical solutions he already owned. He'd done extensive research into how to prep the glass and develop the photo.

Before he opened the bottles, he opened the window a little wider. The chemicals made him dizzy. He'd learned this on his wedding day nearly fifty years ago when he assisted his father-in-law, a professional photographer and collector of all things photography, film, and "moving pictures." Out on the street corner, Earl's beautiful bride positioned herself under the light post. His father-in-law had insisted that the wedding photos be as unique as the couple, and since the man was paying for the wedding, Earl and Margaret had agreed.

Earl helped Margaret's father prepare every antique camera the man owned, most with film and flash bulbs. One with a glass plate. They placed the cameras on tripods all around the wedding venue, the banquet area, and on the cobblestone street underneath the town's primitive lamppost. Earl thought the location a bit cliché since most folks had their photos taken near the old lamp, but the glass plate camera was in play, so maybe it would turn out okay.

Unique.

He could remember the way Margaret's dress moved in the warm breeze, the white lace hugged her arms and traveled down past her wrist, pointing to the diamond ring that glistened on her finger...

What a day that was. Fresh spring air blessed their outdoor ceremony. Margaret was the love of his life. He could never, ever love another. But the couple never got a chance to see how they'd get along. They never had a chance to live out the dreams they'd spent hours planning for on her front porch swing when he came to court her.

They never got to meet their children.

Struck by the sudden wave of memories, Earl sat the chemical solutions on the table with trembling hands and took a step back. This could be the exact camera from that day out on the street. A chill ran down his back and he wondered, ever so briefly, if he should be messing with any of it.

He dismissed the doubt and continued with his project. This size of camera should have a tripod, but none of Earl's tripods would fit this model. A stack of antique atlases would have to do for the time being. He doublechecked the glass plate for scratches or dust. Any such thing would show up in the final product. He poured the solution over the plate, placed the plate in a shoebox and covered it with the lid. It needed total darkness to begin the coating process.

This is a test, he told himself. *To see if the camera works.*

He found a spot across the sidewalk, a neighbor's burning bush in bad need of a trim. In the fall, its leaves turned a fiery red and glowed like embers before the first heavy frost would hit and send the red flames all over the street. In June, though, the bush was nothing spectacular. Just greenery to aim his lens at. He positioned the camera, propped by the atlases, and made sure the curtain wouldn't get in the way.

He carefully loaded the glass plate into the metallic frame attached to the back of the camera and closed it tight. He only had a few moments before the plate would dry completely and be useless, and he didn't have an abundance of supplies to fiddle with.

He checked and doublechecked the sidewalk from the window to make sure it was empty of people.

He meticulously aimed the lens at the bush, took a deep breath and removed the lens cap.

He began to count to twenty, the amount of time it would take for the exposure to be complete.

One one thousand, two one thousand, three one thousand—

Sparks flew from the brass plate. A few of them landed in his white beard, sending the smell of singed hair to join with the stale pipe tobacco.

"I'll be a…" He turned the camera around, quickly replaced the lens cap and pulled out the plate holder, which Earl nearly dropped because it was so hot.

He quickly placed the glass inside the shoebox and applied the final chemical wash, though he didn't think it would do any good. He'd only had a few seconds of exposure before the brass engraving reared its ugliness, not nearly enough time for a proper test.

After a few minutes, he pulled the plate from the box. The image was cloudy, but he could tell right away that he did not capture the burning bush across the street.

He'd captured a boy in a field.

A very surprised young boy.

CHAPTER 9

HEDGE GATHERS himself after a stunned moment. He meets me at the edge of the field and we both run as fast as we can into the shelter of the corn. We don't speak, nor do we stop longer than a second or two to catch our breath—not until we reach the edge of the field near the tractor lane where, much to our surprise, we are not alone.

"What in the good earth's name are you boys doing?"

I recognize the gravelly voice, the same one that had traveled down the air vent and thundered in my ears at the meeting this morning. Now I have an angry face to put with the name. The man is at least a hundred years older than Granddad, according to the wrinkles and leathery skin. Deep furrows line his forehead, cheeks, and even his chin. His skin is so tanned he can almost pass as a descendant of the Miami Indians who'd lived in these parts long ago. His coveralls are stained with tractor grease. Sweat drops trickle from his bald head, following the furrows in his face and exit the tip of his weathered chin.

"We, we…were hiking."

"Hiking. Uh-huh. What did you see on this *hike*?" The old farmer hooks each of his crooked thumbs into his suspender straps on his overalls. We stare wild-eyed at the old man.

"Nothin' much. We saw nothin'."

"Yeah," Hedge finally chimes in. "We got tired of being all cut up by the corn, so we decided to turn around and come home. Never made it much past the tractor lane."

I wince. I hate lying. Yet another reason my stomach churns, but I can only imagine the fate that awaits us back at the house if Granddad catches wind of what we've been up to.

"Well, boys, on the other side of this here field is nothing to explore. Not one thing. Eddie and I don't want no trespassers stomping up our crops." Then, he directs his cold glare at me. "I'm gonna let your grandfather know about this, Oliver."

I stand a little straighter—though I'm not sure how given my weak knees and terrified spine—and meet the man's stare. "I'm sorry sir. It won't happen again." My heart thumps and I hope the direct apology means something. I'd rather go another round with the post in the field than Mr. Deep Throat.

We run all the way to the edge of Granddad's yard before collapsing in the grass. The blades crunch in the heat beneath us, but they are nowhere near as painful as the corn's blades.

"Now what?" I hope Hedge had a bright idea.

"Don't know."

"If he tells Granddad, we're dead." My gut lets out a long, loud gurgle.

"Don't puke. Catch your breath and go in the house like nothing happened." Hedge starts to stand and I notice a patch of drying blood around his neckline.

"Hey, you must've got cut pretty bad, too." I reach to touch my own cheek where the corn had no doubt sliced through a blasted patch of freckles.

"Must've been moving so fast I didn't even feel it. Running through a field of samurai swords would've been more productive."

"You watch too much TV."

"If you'd be happy with TV, we'd not be in this mess." Hedge brushes the dried grass off his pants and tries to wipe the blood from his collar. "I'm heading home before Mom gets off work and hauls me to the ER or something. Or therapy. She'd probably take me back to therapy." Hedge rolls his eyes and holds up his hands to mimic talking mouths. That had been a dark time for him, but his mom swore it had helped Hedge cope with life. I'm not sure how he copes any differently now than before all those sessions that cut into most of our afternoons the previous summer. "Let me know what happens."

I wave to Hedge and gather my backpack. I'll have to dump the pack later to sort out clothes from undone homework from smashed Oreos.

At the house, I see Granddad talking with someone in an old pickup. I'm still sweating from the sprint out of the corn, clammy and weak. As I come closer, I see the driver.

Deep Throat.

The codger is ratting me out already.

I run up to my room, knowing Granddad will soon storm up the stairs to lecture me about being in the field. I'm not sure which old man down in the driveway I'm more intimidated by.

I crack the window open to see if I can hear the men talking.

"… sure Hedge was with him, yes?" Granddad was saying.

Deep Throat guy nods.

"I'll make a phone call or two, dig the contract out of the cabinet, and it'll be okay. Oliver's been through quite a bit. I'll set the boys down and give them a talking to."

I gulp and sulk onto my bed. *Set the boys down* doesn't sound like fun—at all. I've disobeyed. And lied. And, at a time like this, when everyone was stressed out, and after seeing Granddad waving his shotgun the other day—my stomach can't handle much more of this.

I hear more bits of the discussion.

"Chicago can't wait. I saw that green glow from the post the other day and again this afternoon. Someone's been messin' with some gadget out there. We gotta get to the bottom of this."

"Tend to your crops, Jerry. I'll deal with it."

Jerry. That's his name.

"You should know what we stand to lose. You of all people." Jerry Deep Throat mutters some obscenities and starts the pickup, throwing gravel as he backs out of the drive.

I shut the window and flop down again. At least Granddad had left the AC on and the cool air dries some of the sweat.

Chicago. Lawyer. Cabinet. My head spins from the day's events as I try to process what I'd heard. And what I'd done.

More clues I can do nothing about. The only cabinet I know about other than the ones in the kitchen is in farthest corner of the basement surrounded by old National Geographic magazines and wicker laundry baskets the mice had chewed holes through. No way was I going to risk another—

"Oliver!" Granddad's voice scales the stairs like a mighty wave. "Get down here."

My heart takes refuge in my throat. I can barely drag myself to the staircase. Granddad stands at the bottom, looking up with a frown. "You see something out in the field today?"

I didn't dare lie this time. I can only nod. If I speak I'll burst into tears.

Granddad leans on the bottom banister, nods and picks at his fingernails. At least he isn't wielding a shotgun. "Anything happen at the post?" Granddad *knows.* He knows we'd found the secret light post.

"A flash." I choke out the words.

"Anyone nearby other than the two of you boys?"

I shake my head adamantly, as if that will help my case. "No. Me and Hedge."

"How close were you when the flash went off?"

Granddad's now-calm demeanor causes me to relax a bit. "Not close at all. We didn't touch it." *Half true.*

"Good. We'll talk more about this later. Stay out of the fields. Jerry's irate. We don't need any more trouble. No one else is to know. Understand?"

"Yessir."

Granddad walks away, but I'm frozen and my mind whirls.

I hear his old blue pickup spring to life and pull down the lane. I stand motionless, my feet stuck at the top of the stairs. That was it? Maybe this wasn't a big deal after all. But it had to be. Granddad had threatened Mom and Dad if they left.

I convince my legs to carry me to the basement after five minutes of stone-cold stillness. They shake and wobble down the steps. I know I should listen to them. My legs have the better idea of staying put upstairs rather than risking a second trip under the house. I push the thought of another confrontation with Granddad out of my head and press on.

On my way down the steps, I dial each of my parents' phones and neither answers. No surprise. They had no idea what went on here today, and maybe they never would. Dad had promised Granddad that he'd call every day to check on me and to give updates on the progress between him and Mom, but that hasn't happened. For all I know, Dad hasn't even found Mom yet.

Or maybe Dad didn't want to.

I reach the corner with the buried metal filing cabinet. The bare bulb with the pull-string switch barely lights the area near the washer, and the rays don't quite make it all the way to the back of the basement. I'll need to put everything back the way I find it to avoid another blowout with Granddad.

I move baskets and enough of the magazines to reach the rusting cabinet which had been propped up on cylinder blocks. I open the top drawer. Envelopes and folders marked "PAID," "TAXES" and "BILLS" cram it full. The second drawer holds more of the same. Each time I close a drawer, I run to the filmed-up window and stand on the overturned bucket to listen for Granddad's truck.

I have to move a few more Nat Geos to reach the third drawer, which is locked, or jammed at the very least.

I rummage near the washer for the pocketknife I'd accidentally sent through the wash the weekend before and hadn't bothered to take back upstairs. The blade slips easily between the drawer and the old cabinet's casing, and the drawer pops open.

One more quick listen at the bucket for the truck and another listen at the foot of the stairs for footsteps before I feel it's safe to continue.

I pull out a stack of photos. I turn on the flashlight of Hedge's old cell phone to inspect them more closely.

Granddad and Granny on their wedding day. Granny holding Dad as a baby. With me as a baby. Me and Billy in front of the barn. I remember Mom had insisted we "pretend to like each other" for that photo.

There were too many to look through, but I wonder why they aren't in frames or an album instead of stuffed in a drawer to be the next victims of a basement flood.

Under the photos is a brown file, stained with coffee mug rings and purple sticky spots. I smile at these. That was grape jelly from Granddad's favorite breakfast. I had heard Granny argue and fuss over the mess Granddad left after such a breakfast many times.

I carefully open the file and find a page marked "last known activity" in bad handwriting. An address in Chicago is barely readable—I see now I've gotten my bad penmanship through genetics.

With the phone, I snap a photo of the address and hope it's clear enough to read. I am about to replace everything when I notice something hanging at the very back of the drawer. Whatever it is has become partially stuck in the sliding mechanism of the drawer above it. I give it a tug as gravel pings against metal outside.

I panic, place the new-found paper deep in my pocket and shove the folder, photos, and drawer back into place. I replace the piles of rotting magazines and baskets as best I can and bound over to the washing machine to switch the load into the dryer as Granddad comes halfway down the steps.

"Doin' okay?"

"Yeah. Just getting clothes for school washed up." *Another half-truth.*

"Hurry up. I brought back dinner."

I slam the dryer door shut for effect and head up the steps, doublechecking the mystery paper is tucked safely in my pocket.

Safely in the pocket where it and the photo on the phone burn a hole in my brain all the way through Darla's Diner fried chicken dinner to-go with all the greasy fixin's.

CHAPTER 10

UPSTAIRS, I call Hedge with the news.

"You want to what?" Hedge crunches and slurps into the phone. No doubt replenishing the massive amount of burnt calories from sprinting through the corn in the heat.

"I found an address in the city. I think that the answers to this mess are there."

"And just how," Hedge pauses to take a wet swallow, "are you gonna get all the way to Chicago?"

Fallston is rural Illinois, but not too rural. Somewhat isolated, but not too far away from the big city. Those who live in Fallston choose to do so on purpose—and those who'd thought they'd love the change of pace from the busy Chicago chaos were usually mistaken. Those like Mom who would fast-foot it back to the city at the first sign of boredom—even if there wasn't trouble to run from.

"Well, we'd need help. I was thinking about calling Billy."

"*We* need help? And for crying out loud, Oliver! Billy?" Hedge has never met Billy, and he'd told me that he never wanted to, either.

"Right now I'm more scared of Granddad and the old codgers than I am Billy." I lay my head back on the bed and toss a pair of balled-up socks at the ceiling.

"I see. Well, why do I have to go?"

"Because you *know* about this Hedge. Because those old farmers don't want us to know about this. Because this could destroy my family. Because I need your help." I pause. There is only silence from Hedge's end of the line. I feel hopelessness welling up in my chest and am near tears again. How quickly I can go from confident schemer to scared little kid…

I think about the week ahead and about tomorrow. The eighth-grade state Government field trip to Chicago. The field trip that informally marks the passing from middle school to high school, which, in our small town means taking classes in one building farther down the parking lot from the one we're in now. Hedge has been complaining about this trip since the end of seventh grade.

"And because," I add, "you can skip the class field trip tomorrow."

I swallow the lump in my throat. *Back to schemer again.* The plan forms bit by bit as the tears pull themselves back behind my eyelids, and excitement replaces the rib-crushing desperation. Bit by bit, step by step, I see a way to the answers.

Another slurp. "Skip the trip? What's the plan?" Hedge is all in.

"We'll talk tomorrow. I gotta go before Granddad overhears." I flip the phone shut and grab my notebook.

With Hedge on board all I have to do now is call Billy.
Billy.

I sprint down the stairs to the bathroom and throw up Darla's fried chicken with all the fixin's.

CHAPTER 11

EARL TURNED the developed photo over and over in his hand. He knew the street had been empty when he'd taken the photo.

He'd been so careful to ensure it was empty.

The camera's bronze plate had cooled and seemed stable for now. He didn't remember sparks when the photos were taken on his wedding day. But, then again, he wasn't waiting for anything but the wedding night.

Earl ran his time-worn fingers through his gray beard which was in bad need of a trim. He'd deal with that later. He had put off quite a bit of self-care in the last few days. He'd been so preoccupied with his new find.

He laid the photo near the atlases and sat back in his red armchair. Margaret had called it his "smoking seat." Earl loved sitting with a good book and smoking his pipe. She had teased him about getting a smoking jacket, but that seemed too frivolous; the money was better spent on good tobacco.

He was tired. How long had he searched for an object bearing the bronze plate? How many antique stores and flea markets? How many estate sales and auctions? How many hours had he poured over newspapers and ancestries to track down the tiniest bits of information? And now he had another enigma.

Where was that boy? *When* was he?

The boy's clothes appeared modern enough, but boys of that age had been wearing T-shirts for almost as long as he could remember. Earl had never worn a T-shirt, not in public anyway. It didn't feel right. He was more comfortable in a button-up and vest.

Earl pulled a brass magnifying glass from the side-table drawer and examined the photo. The boy's shirt had no writing that he could tell. No name of a school or a town. He couldn't make out any logos. For all Earl knew, that kid could be in South Africa.

And no sign of his neighbor's burning bush at all.

There was, he thought, the tiniest hint of something human off to the side, away from the boy. An elbow, or the very tip of someone's fingers, perhaps. A hand. As if reaching out to the mystery boy near the post. Maybe someone *was* trying to warn the boy.

To save him.

Or maybe those weren't fingertips at all.

Earl tossed the photo and glass slide into the drawer with the magnifying glass. Dealing with daily frustrations he could handle. Being this close and yet having more questions than answers—well, that was another matter.

He took a deep breath as he watched out the window at the slow pace of the neighbors coming and going from who knows where, the cool of the evening beckoning them. Walking dogs. Taking kids to the park. Living normal lives.

He could try again. He had film and enough chemicals left for one more try. Or, he could wait for Gabe or the antique store lady to call him with news of another find from his list—which would most likely be dead ends. The camera was no doubt the find of the century. The find of *his* lifetime, anyway.

Earl snatched the photo out of the drawer again, drawn by its mystery and fueled by frustration. He hoped no harm came to this boy, whoever he was. Earl had meant no harm at all. His dull blue eyes welled up with tears as he peered into the boy's face. Seems like his old eyeballs did that a lot these days. He'd blame it, in front of others, on aging and allergies. Secretly, he'd shed more tears than should be allowed a man for one lifetime—or maybe two.

He had tried with everything in his soul to solve this problem. To make things right.

Maybe it was time to give up. He glanced over his shoulder toward the bedroom as the moaning once again flooded under the closed door and crept up his spine. The hollowness he had felt so many times consumed his core, and his limbs felt heavy with burden.

Maybe it was time to call it done.

Earl was just so very tired.

CHAPTER 12

THE TRIP to Chicago for government class is one of the least-looked forward to trips of the entire educational life for the students in Fallston. Not one kid that had gone before me had ever enjoyed packing a brown-bag lunch and bouncing on the bus all the way to the city. Not one kid paid attention to the guide or learned anything or profited in any way, shape, or form from this rite of passage—or so the complaining in the halls went after all the previous eighth-grade classes had returned.

And the bellyaching would go on for the whole week after the trip. The only bright spot would be if some kid got motion sick on the bus and blew chunks in a preppy girl's hair. That had happened at least twice.

Even the staff didn't like the trip, and no one knew why the school kept the tradition up. The bus drivers had to be paid overtime because most of the boys were, well, teen boys and would try to cause a ruckus to combat the boredom that blanketed the trip. The poor parent chaperones always had that deer-in-the-headlights stare.

I feel sorry for sweet Mrs. Lakes. She has been assigned as volunteer parent for the day; her daughter Olivia is in my class, and Mrs. Lakes will be our group's chaperone. Normally, I'd be uber respectful and follow along at her elbow for the entire tour. I don't want to get the lady in trouble, but I have business to take care of.

Today I have to be someone different.

The call to Billy late last night had gone about as well as I had expected. It would have cost Billy less than five bucks to pick us up from the bus parking lot at the government building and drive us to the address I'd discovered in the basement cabinet.

I still have the cash Dad had left me for the phone, and that was all I had to offer. Taking a cab would only get us one way, and caught for sure. I took a big risk trusting that Billy would show up. But, Billy hates hard work, and easy money was easy money.

"What are you up to, brat?" I thought Billy sounded different. High on drugs maybe. This was so stupid.

"Not your business. You want the money or not?"

"Yeah, whatever."

"How's Mom? And by the way, she doesn't know about this, okay? I don't want to stress her out."

"Don't know how Mom is. Haven't seen her for weeks now."

That realization—that Mom hadn't spoken to her precious Billy— was almost as hard to swallow as anything else I'd learned Sunday.

"What?" I had tried to hide the panic in my voice. "I thought she was with you."

"Not for weeks. I thought she was living large at Fabulous Farm."

I didn't retaliate. Granddad had mentioned how she was probably staying with Billy until things with Dad either came to a head or came to a close. I hoped Dad would have called me if there were problems. But I guess that would be unlikely, too.

I continued. "We need picked up at ten tomorrow."

"Whatever."

As I replayed the conversation to Hedge before we boarded the bus, we were only half sure this shaky plan will work. But, it was the only plan I could come up with. To *do* something. To help mend the family and stay on the farm.

Granddad had left the farm in his old pickup for Chicago way before my bus left the school lot, destined for the same city. I hope the chores of the farm will call Granddad back from his business he'd discussed with Jerry long before the bus brings us home.

I hope we don't miss the bus home…

Chicago is massive, but the fear of bumping into him or Mom makes the metropolis shrink to the size of a minimart. Not to mention the fear of Billy squealing.

The bus ride is miserable and reeks of lukewarm lunches. Sam Mason intentionally brought tuna and left it out of the community cooler to gross everyone out. I'm glad the other kids don't pay much attention to me or Hedge. It will make today a little easier. We barely speak on the trip. We'd talked everything out last night and this morning. Better to play it safe and stay quiet. I glance at my co-conspirator. Hedge, earbuds in and zoned out the window, doesn't seem nervous at all.

Must be nice.

The bus finally pulls into the lot at the government building. There are a dozen long yellow transports already here from other schools— poor tortured souls. There will be a big crowd, and that is a blessing today.

The teachers divide up the kids with the volunteer parents, clip- boards and nametags in hand, to help control the flow of the day. There aren't enough teachers for each group since Mr. Stewart "came down with the flu" two days earlier. His group, hand-picked to be led by the timid Mrs. Lakes, contains Hedge, me, Olivia, and three other outcasts. These particular kids aren't troublemakers and wouldn't require the extra adult.

Guilt pricks the back of my neck.

Mrs. Lakes does a quick head count after the we get our tickets. The groups from my school and several others are elbow-to-elbow, mixing and moving like a confused amoeba. "Ready children? Let's stay together now. Pick a buddy." Mrs. Lakes would have been more suited for preschoolers at a petting zoo than this.

"Ready, buddy?" Hedge whispers close to my ear. I nod. Hedge is grinning, ready for adventure, adrenaline no doubt surging through his videogame-addicted brain.

We allow the others in the group to walk the closest to our fearless leader. We duck to the side of a ticket booth as the rest cross into the entrance. We casually walk across the lobby, weaving in and out of students from other schools and make our way back to the bus unnoticed by anyone. Our driver had remained in the bus, AC running (it wasn't his dime paying for the gas) and is reading a newspaper.

"Mr. Burn," I say in the best good-kid voice I can muster. "Would you let us in? We forgot something and Mrs. Lakes sent us back to get it." I hate lying. Probably comes from being lied to so often. I justify it; it was, after all, my last year of middle school. What would they do? Suspend me through high school?

The bus driver opens the door all the way barely looking up from his paper. We slide to the back where we gather our packs filled with water, maps, and snacks. Hedge has a smartphone with a GPS, but I like the maps better. We thank the driver who, again not looking up from his paper, closes the door behind us.

I hope we won't be missed until lunchtime when the rest of the class would gather in the parking lot to eat from the coolers. By then, it would be too late to do anything but call the parents. And by the time the parents could do anything, I hope Billy will have dropped us back at the lot in time to explain how we'd "gotten lost" and had to call my brother for help.

Weak, I know. But it's the best I have.

This is the last week of school, so Hedge and I would only have to endure a few days of discipline. The plan catches up with my abdomen and I groan. After thinking this through for the hundredth time, the holes in my grand scheme light up like runway lights, causing my head to spin.

"You sure Billy will show?"

I'm not sure about anything. "No. If he doesn't, we'll take a cab. If he does and rats us out, well, we'll be no worse off than we were if we had got caught in the parking lot just now." We wait at the intersection for Billy.

Billy had moved to Chicago years ago at Granddad's insistence after he had caught Billy bullying me. Actually, bullying was an understatement, but that was what the juvenile court had labeled it, so everyone in the family did, too. It was more like torture. The fact that I need Billy now sets my teeth on edge.

Hedge looks at his watch for the tenth time as Billy pulls up in an old, beat-up Volkswagen. I shake my head at Hedge and take a step back, but Hedge pushes me forward. "Too late to back out now, freak."

"Get in, morons." Billy nods to the back seat and holds out his hand. "Money. Address. Now. I've got better things to do."

I push a wad of cash toward Billy. He still cuts his blond hair close enough to see the freckles on his scalp, I guess he cuts it himself for lack of funds. Despite his slight frame, he still has height and quite a few pounds on me. And, because of our history, I hate to admit it, but I'm truly terrified of him.

He grabs my wrist hard, twisting until I'm pulled forward over the seatback and my ear is nearly in Billy's mouth. His breath reeks of rotten eggs. "What's this about, creep?"

I strain to keep my voice calm. "What's it to you? You got the money." Billy shoves me back to my seat, glances at the address and takes off, tires squealing.

Hedge, white-faced, leans in close. "Seat belts highly recommended. You okay?"

I buckle and nod. I stare out the window, massaging my sore wrist. Hedge leans his forehead on the window and grips the hand rest until his knuckles go white. He occasionally glances at me, and I can see the grease smudge left on the window from his sweaty brow.

The address is about twenty minutes away from the bus lot. Too far to go on foot in both directions, and my mind struggles to figure a way back to the school group that doesn't involve Billy.

The Volkswagen sputters to a stop outside a tall, slender house on a quiet street. I double-check the address to be sure Billy isn't pulling something. The tiny bit of landscaping is neatly trimmed. An ornate, black handrail lines the steps leading to an ominous wooden door which seems larger than the house itself. Lacy white curtains blow gently from the front window. Someone is probably home if the windows are open.

"Can you be back in two hours?" I ask.

"Got more money?" Billy sneers.

"Yes. I've got more for the trip back, you sick—"

Hedge grabs my arm. "We need him to get us back."

"I'll be here. But if you don't tell me what this is about, I'll tell Mom."

"I would expect nothing less from you, Billy."

I'd nearly vomited back in the parking lot when Billy pulled up. Now I'm mouthing off to him. I feel like two people are fighting for control over my very being.

We get out and the Bug pulls away from the curb. A hand out the window shows the whole street an obscene gesture as Billy drives off.

"You think he'll be back?" Hedge stares down the road.

"He wants more money. He's probably broke."

"You got more money? I thought you gave all you had?"

"No. But Billy doesn't need to know that until he gets us back to the bus."

"Yeah." Hedge rubs his neck and adjusts his backpack. "That's a smart plan. That way, he can beat us both up in front of our entire class. Now I think *I'm* gonna hurl."

I turn toward the little house. "Yeah. We're probably screwed." We climb the steps and I grasp the ring in the mouth of the lion-head door knocker. It might as well be a living, breathing great cat, the way my hand shakes. Whatever comes next I deserve. All the lying and stealing and manipulating I've done to get here. I've earned every bit of the bile in my throat and a set of missing fingers if it comes to it.

I knock the heavy iron ring against the door three times then take a giant step backward, almost knocking Hedge off the stoop. Hedge pushes back. "Watch it! Who do ya think's gonna be on the other side? Satan?"

The massive door creaks open and I hold my breath.

CHAPTER 13

DUMB KIDS.

Billy could see those morons googling at him from the rearview mirror as he drove away. They're probably meeting their dealer. Or buying a gun.

But that didn't make any sense. Oliver had always been the "good kid."

The favorite.

The perfect baby.

They shared the same mom, and Billy was ten when Oliver was born. Things grew worse with the favoritism over the years. He could see how much Mom and her new husband just *loved* baby Oliver. Even now, after all these years, he could feel sparks of jealous rage. His own dad ditched him and Mom to go "grab a smoke" and never came back. What a cliché.

Then he had to share Mom with Jim.

Then he had to share her with the baby.

It was all too much. Secretly he dreamed Mom was putting on an act and that she really did love Billy more. He was her firstborn son, after all. She should love him more than anyone in the world…

Billy slowed the car. No, it didn't make sense. What could those two dweebs want at that old house?

He took a right turn and rounded the block. It wasn't as if he had a big, important life to rush off to. Not like he had a job. The fifty bucks that Oliver handed him would have to put gas in the Bug and food in his stomach until he could find another temp job.

Maybe in surveillance.

Billy thought he was decent at spying. He'd spied on Mom and Jim and Oliver many times over the years. "Granddad" never did like him, so Billy didn't give a hoot what that old geezer did. He wasn't even blood relation.

The others, though. They never knew he was watching.

He pulled the car over a half block from where he dropped the boys. They must have gone into the house, as they weren't on the street twiddling their thumbs. He cut the engine and leaned his seat back. He had to pick them up here in two hours anyway. He may as well wait as to drive around wasting gas.

He rummaged through the clutter on the floor and found a half box of Cracker Jacks. That'd have to do. If he did land a job as a private detective, he'd have to buy a less conspicuous car. One that blended in. He threw a handful of stale caramel corn into his mouth.

He could catch drug dealers and cheaters and thieves. He'd take his pay straight up, or he could blackmail his marks and play them against one another.

Billy grinned at his fantasy as he used his tongue to dislodge a kernel from his back tooth. He'd probably need a high-tech camera with—

His daydream was cut short at the sight of a black sedan with dark, tinted windows parking in the opposite direction. Billy thought it was smart to lower the seat a bit more to stay out of view.

That's the kind of car I need. It blends.

The driver stepped out dressed in jeans and a black AC/DC shirt. His hair matched the car, jet black and slicked back. His face was eggshell white.

Drug dealer.

Billy called it. He fist-bumped the roof of his bug. He could call Granddad right now and rat Oliver out.

Billy watched intently and had to keep adjusting his half-broken seat to get the best views. The driver walked across the street to an older vehicle parked in front of Oliver's drop point. The man reached into his back pocket, looked up and down the road, and bent near the car's rear bumper. He stood, stretched, walked back to his car, and got inside.

Billy waited. As soon as the guy left, he'd go find the stash and have proof that Oliver was using. Or dealing. Where else would Oliver get fifty bucks?

He dug around on the floor for something to grab the drugs with, so he wouldn't leave his own fingerprints on the stash. Billy grinned again. See, he could be just as smart as Oliver.

Billy tossed the now-empty Cracker Jack box back to its original spot. It'd only been a few minutes since he dropped off the boys, and, much to his dismay, the drug dealer never started his black sedan. Instead, the driver's window cracked and tiny spirals of smoke wafted out. More and more minutes passed.

It was hot in the Volkswagen, and the stale snack had made him thirsty. Billy wondered if Pale Face was an undercover cop. What if Granddad already figured the whole thing out and already called the cops? Maybe Billy should cut his losses and rat out the boys now. He struggled to figure out which tactic would do Oliver more damage.

He had spare change enough for a pay phone, and it would be worth every red cent to watch Granddad rain fire down on Oliver's head.

He started his car and pulled into the street, careful to get a good look at the drug dealer/undercover cop's black car. As Billy passed, Pale Face rolled down the tinted window the rest of the way and stared straight into Billy's eyes.

Billy thought he'd seen the Devil.

CHAPTER 14

THE OLD MAN looks as startled to see us as we are to see him. Hedge and I stare at him and he stares back for a long moment before anyone speaks.

The man is dressed like something out of an old Sherlock Holmes movie, complete with cane, white beard, and a three-piece suit. An old suit. Not like anything I'd ever seen anyone wear outside of a movie before.

"May I help you?" The old man asks, not taking his eyes off Hedge. I glance between my friend and the strange man on the stoop. I'm not sure what Hedge did to gain the old guy's interest—or suspicion.

"Yessir. We've come a long way to see you. It's a long story, and we only have a little bit—"

The man stands up tall and straightens his vest. "I'd be delighted to hear your long story. Would you like some lemonade?" *Unreal.* Hedge and I shrug and nod. "Come in, please." He holds the door open wide and we follow him inside. Past the point of no return. The man turns to us. "Just wait here for a moment, please."

The old man disappears into another room, his cane clicks on the hardwood floor. We hear him rustling paper, opening and closing doors, and such. I look around. Old paintings of ships and landscapes and fancy dinner plates with dainty floral patterns hang in the entryway. The place smells of tobacco—not nasty cigarettes, but sweeter and almost comforting.

"Probably hiding the Do-It-Yourself-Poison-Making Kit from Mad Scientist Monthly. I don't think I'm drinking his lemonade." Hedge runs his finger along a portrait of a wrinkled old lady wearing spectacles.

"Shut up and be nice." I still can't process why this guy let us in. No questions asked. I'd had no expectations of what would be behind the door, but I never expected the occupant to be eager to speak with us.

"My name is Earl." The old man gives a slight bow and a nod to us as he comes back to the entryway. "I apologize for my rudeness. Had to tidy up a bit; it's been a long while since we've, uh, since I've had any guests. Come right this way."

"I *bet* it's been a while," Hedge smiles. I give him a quick elbow to the gut.

We follow Earl into a living room. Several cushioned chairs and a flowered sofa circle a threadbare oriental rug. A table filled with stacks of dusty hardback books sits under the window. The frilly lace curtains I'd seen from Billy's car blow over the top of the stacks, sending little tufts of dust into the air. The tobacco aroma is stronger in this room.

"Do you mind?" Earl points toward a pipe. We shake our heads in unison. Earl lights the pipe, sits back in a well-worn, red chair, and crosses his legs. He reaches up and runs his ancient fingers through his beard, which nearly reaches his chest bone.

"Now, please. Tell me your names and your story. And, if you're truly in a hurry," he takes a long draw on his pipe, "do please leave out the boring bits." Earl grins as smoke billows around his head. He points his pipe toward the lemonade on the oval coffee table in front of us. "And always use a coaster, please." He glances over his shoulder toward a closed door behind his chair.

We start the tale slowly at first, mostly about my family junk. We gain speed as we reach the point where we hid in the basement. Sometimes we trip over one another with interruptions and corrections. The old man listens patiently. Occasionally, he glances over his shoulder at the closed door behind him. He takes long draws from the pipe while the smoke curls in the air and falls around his chair like ribbons.

"And that's how we got here. I know you probably don't believe us. And you may not know anything about it, but I, I—" I trail off with a shrug. There isn't anything else I can do or say but wait for the old man's reaction. I glance at my watch—only thirty minutes left until Billy would be back to take us to the bus lot.

I shift on the plush couch cushion and press my arm tight against my stomach.

Earl sets the pipe on the small table by his chair. On the side of the table is a small handle shaped like a mini version of the lion-head door knocker. Earl pulls it open and takes out a flat square of something. He rises from his chair with the help of his cane and slowly makes his way across the room. Keeping eye contact with me, he hands Hedge the square.

Hedge glances at it. "It's a photo." Then he looks closer. And closer. Until his nose almost touches the print. "Are you kidding me?" He shoves the square into my hand.

I look down. After processing the image, I toss the thick photo onto the coffee table. The photo shows Hedge's face from the day we discovered the post.

"I'm afraid you boys have stumbled onto a conundrum that I've spent my whole life trying to solve." The old guy's pale blue eyes brim with tears and he uses both hands to lean heavily on his cane. "And I believe I may have brought great danger to you, young Hedge. For that, I am truly sorry."

Hedge goes pale. "What do you mean 'great danger'? And skip the boring bits, please. We're in a hurry." I elbow Hedge in the gut again, but not as hard this time. I'm likely as pale as he is.

Earl sits back in his red chair and nods, a grim look spreads across his face. "Hedge, have you been feeling ill? Anything out of the normal since the day under the light?"

Hedge thinks for a second. "Well, come to think of it, I can't sleep too good. When I shut my eyes, all I can see are green flashes. The light threw sparks and I thought I may have hurt my eyes."

"That's how it starts, I'm afraid."

"How *what* starts?" I look frantically between Hedge and Earl. "Should he see a doctor?"

"I'm terribly afraid that won't be of help."

Hedge leaps up. "Look, I don't know what's going on, but I'm outta here. I'm—"

A pounding at the front door stops Hedge's rant. Whoever it is clearly isn't using the knocker; they're using fists and shouting. My heart skids to a stop then starts again, throbbing in my ears. It sounds like—

Earl motions us to stay put and makes his way to the door. "I say, what's the trouble, sir?"

I can hear the men in the entry, but before I can stand or think, a very angry Granddad appears in the living room.

CHAPTER 15

I LEAP TO ATTENTION, standing shoulder to shoulder with Hedge. Over the last few days, the last couple of years, really, I've struggled in that limbo somewhere between childhood and adulthood. In this moment, however, I am firmly a child. A terrified little boy, to be exact.

"Billy called me. What do you think you're doing, Oliver?" Granddad's voice shakes dust from the aged picture frames hanging on the wall.

I can't hold back the tears. I sob in great gulps into my shirt sleeve. Right here in the strange man's living room. Right here in front of Hedge and Earl and Granddad. I come up for just enough air to reply "Trying to fix it all," before burying my face in my hands.

I feel an arm around me and notice the familiar comfort of Granddad's overalls—part aftershave, part gasoline from the tractor. When I dare to glance up, Granddad's face is soft. His embrace feels better than anything I can remember in a long time.

"I'm so sorry, Son. I'm so sorry. I *warned* you to stay away from the field. I've been warning you your whole life. I tried so hard to protect you from this."

Earl takes a step closer. "Sir, would you like to have a seat and perhaps something to drink? I think we could all do with a little more time together, if you don't mind."

Granddad pulls away from me and gives Hedge's dark hair a quick tousle. "Okay. Let me step outside to call Oliver's teacher and Hedge's mom first."

"Do they gotta know, Mr. Andrews? 'Cause Mom's gonna kill me and call Dad and then—" Hedge's eyes flashed fear. I know he must be thinking another round with the therapist is looming.

"I'm afraid so. And, by the way, Oliver. This is not what I meant when I said you should have an adventure." A stern glance from Granddad causes both of us to bow our heads in humble regret and retreat to the sofa in defeat.

Our host busies himself in the kitchen with more lemonade and, this time, he presents us with a silver tray filled with miniature cakes in squares and circles.

Hedge brightens a bit. "Looks like Ding Dongs and Twinkies all chopped up."

Earl smiles. "Eat up. You may be here a little longer than you think. If you need a washroom, young Oliver, I'll show you where it is."

I nod. It would be nice to get the tears and snot cleaned up before going any further down the rabbit hole that is now my life.

Earl leads me through the narrow hall to a minuscule bathroom. The toilet and sink are almost on top of each other, but it's clean. I splash cold water on my face and dry it off with a hand towel Earl had left me. My eyes are bloodshot. My freckles light up with extra orange pigment when I'm upset or cry, making me look like an Oompa Loompa straight from the chocolate factory. I hate that.

I pause in front of the mirror, pushing on the largest freckles high on my cheeks. Thoughts race at lightning speed now. Billy's betrayal. How Granddad got to this place so quickly. The trouble I'll be in at school when I return. Mom and Dad—

Hedge taps on the door. "My turn, bro."

I trade places with him. "Sorry I got you into this mess, Hedge."

Hedge grins. "That's okay. Let's solve this so I can go back to my games. Or geography homework. I need a vacation from this drama."

When he turns to face the mirror, I spot something above Hedge's shirt collar.

"What's on your back?"

Hedge reaches around but can't see or touch the spot. We try looking in the mirror together, but the bathroom is too small for us both. "Looks like some sort of tattoo."

"I must've leaned against something on the bus." Hedge brushes at it, nudges me to the hallway and closes the bathroom door.

When we gather in the living room, Earl speaks first. He stands behind the ornate red chair half blocking the closed door. "I've something to explain." He tells his story of the quest for artifacts with bronze plates, and he moves around to show Granddad the camera. "I'm afraid whoever is near these objects when they are activated—or turned on—is in danger of becoming ill."

Granddad has no expression. I keep waiting for him to laugh or interrupt or get up to leave. But he doesn't. He only says, "I know. I lost my wife to the lamppost in the field." My heart sinks and thoughts whirl again.

Granny? He *knows* about this stuff?

Granddad explains how he and the other farmers had bought up land surrounding the light post through the years, all to protect anyone from getting hurt under the "artifact" as the men described it. "The other families suffered similar losses back in the day. As a matter of fact, I believe the boys got your address because we keep track of those people looking for bronze-plated items." He shot me a disapproving glare.

No wonder Granddad is so adamant about secrets. No wonder he was so rageful when Dad didn't want the land. No wonder—

I look toward Hedge. *Oh no.*

Hedge must've made the connection, too, because he jumps up and runs to the bathroom.

"Wait. Is Hedge going to die?" I weigh a thousand pounds. The realization sunk in deep and sharp.

"Now hold on, we don't know if it always—" Granddad tries to explain.

"Now. I want to know *now*. I need to know." I stand and pace, hands clamped behind my head to keep my brain from spinning. "I've killed my best friend." I fall to my knees.

Earl comes close to offer comfort. I regain control of my muscles and nearly jump in the old man's face. "Is he? Going to die?"

Hedge appears in the doorway, the same question smeared all over his face.

Earl's solemn expression gives little comfort. "I've someone I want you to meet."

He calmly moves to face the door he's been guarding through the whole visit. He glances over his shoulder at the three of us and turns the knob.

Slowly. Gently.

The door creaks open, and I hear a muffled wheeze. A shaky "hello" escapes the depths of the room.

"Pardon our state. She hasn't had visitors in many years." Earl pushes the door open a bit further and motions us to come closer. "Meet Margaret. My wife."

Hedge and I stand in front of Granddad in the doorway of the dimly lit bedroom. The frail woman is almost invisible under the pale blue quilt. Her hair is the same snow-white shade as Earl's beard and lies scattered in all directions around her shoulders. One side of her face looks like any other elderly lady's face. The other side, though…

Earl moves to sit near his wife. He cradles her hand in his and gently kisses her forehead. She tries a smile, but only one side of her lips cooperate. My gut wrenches when she pulls her other arm from under the quilt.

A strange mark glistens on the old woman's wrinkled arm. Even in the dim light, I can make out vining purple strings twisted and tangled like a drunken strand of DNA extending from the bend in her wrist, climbing toward her elbow and then disappearing under the sleeve of her nightgown.

Like the vines on the lamppost.

Like the faint mark now festering on my best friend's neck.

CHAPTER 16

HE'D BEEN WAITING OUTSIDE for a while now. There was more commotion at this tiny house today than there had been in ages—even during those times in the last few months when the ambulance spilled EMTs into the old couple's home. The old gal was getting weaker. You'd think the guy would give up and move on with his life, but love conquers all.

At least that's what they say.

Knox had grown tired of the waiting. He knew the old man had been gaining ground on his quest, but he couldn't sit here forever. At least they had used the same ambulance company for each emergency call. That made tracking the old woman's medical condition fairly simple. Health care was the easiest system of all to hack. These businesses all thought their firewalls and anti-hacking software were state of the art.

They hadn't met Knox. They didn't even know he existed.

Knox squirmed in the seat, trying to relieve the knot in his back. He could have done great things with his genius. Genius always came with a price though. And he wouldn't become part of the system. Not the same system full of grand decision makers who'd made fun, poked, and prodded on him until he bled. Not interested.

The bully in the Volkswagen—Knox could spot a bully from miles away—had made him, he was sure. He'd locked eyes with the schmuck as he'd passed by in his beat-up car. Knox had no idea why the bully was there. Shortly after the Bug pulled away, a rusty blue pickup truck took its place and another old geezer wearing overalls showed up, beating with both fists like an ape on the front door.

And then nothing.

No one had come or gone from the house in over two hours.

He double-checked the tracker under Earl's car from the laptop monitor resting in the passenger's seat. It was working just fine. He wished he'd brought the other tracker; he could have slapped one on that old pickup and made his life a little easier, but he'd have to sit.

And wait.

And watch.

He fiddled with the binoculars, training them to the window, but the curtains obscured everything but major movements, and even those gave him no clues. His mind drifted to his father. Then to his father's father. Then to the ancient journal of ancestors further back. His family had been cursed. Knox was sure of it. Magic, his family had called it.

Others called it witchcraft.

Knox had the grand privilege of witnessing the birth of this current culture where everything had a genetic root and with enough "investigation" an answer could be found.

Truth is, his whole family was burdened with genius, magic or not, and now the rest of the world wanted him stopped. Or exploited.

Well, at least the handful of powerful people that *did* know of Knox's existence.

Cursed.

Nothing more. Nothing less.

To be rid of the curse was not an option. The only way to escape his current misery was to harness his talent and turn it against those who'd hurt him so badly. Those who would continue to hurt him if they could find him. Those like the bully in the Volkswagen and the geezers in the little house across the street.

Knox tossed his binoculars aside and turned on the ignition to get some air moving. He was starting to cool down when the massive oak door opened.

Earl showed Overall Guy down the steps and two disheveled boys followed. Knox had somehow missed the kids. Two very scared looking boys—Knox could spot fear as easily as he could spot a bully.

Perhaps these were family members come to pay respects to the old woman in her last days. But Knox's extensive search of all records showed the old couple had no living family and never had kids of their own.

The old man's guests piled in the pickup as Overall Guy flipped open a cell phone and drove away. Knox had to move quickly as he was facing the wrong direction to tail them smoothly.

He pulled away from the curb at almost the same time as the truck and rounded the block as fast as he dared go without drawing attention. Getting pulled over by some cop with a quota wouldn't help matters. The old pickup, so out of place in neighborhoods like this one, would be easy to spot, but he'd have to catch up and hope the guy was still on the same road.

There. Up ahead, the pickup truck with three bouncing silhouettes sped over the poorly maintained road. Knox breathed out sweet relief, glanced at the stationary GPS dot for Earl's car on his laptop's screen, and settled in for the drive. He'd let a car or two get between him and Overalls, but he would stay close.

He wondered what the three knew. It would be a shame—well, almost a shame—to have to deal with them if they were innocent.

But *Knox* was innocent. He couldn't help what he was.

Innocent people sometimes get hurt.

Especially the weak ones.

CHAPTER 17

"AND YOU'RE SURE ABOUT THIS?"

"Yes, very sure."

The lawyer slumped in his black leather chair. This is not what he'd signed up for. His father and his father before him were all first-class lawyers. It ran in the blood. His office resembled his father's office, and his grandfather's. A fine space where dark cherry bookcases filled with beautiful volumes of law books line the walls. Crystal picture frames, spaced evenly along every other shelf, held happy images of his wife and two children—if only they were true images. He had twice as many photos of his golden Labradors. The Labs were his favorite if he were honest with himself.

One would think by looking at the place that he practiced real law. And he could. And he did.

His dad and grandfather had taken part in the age-old Society that swore allegiances to protect some mythical, magical nonsense. He didn't buy into it, but his grandparents—and possibly even his great grandfather—were sold. Adamantly sold. Like the family fortune disappears and the world comes to an end if you don't join up—and the lawyer's family had quite the fortune.

Which is why he put up with the needy wife and whiny kids.

Images.

Maintain the status.

So the job was passed down to him. To protect his family's inheritance, to serve the greater good, and to protect the clients—mostly grumpy old men—that paid him so well.

"The land must remain with the original families, as stipulated by the original wills and Societal Contract. Blood relation. It makes things much more complicated with more people finding out about the post. This Hedge and Earl, do you think they can be trusted?" The lawyer was on the edge of his seat now. As if that would make old Henry Andrews listen any better.

"They're good and scared. And rightfully so. Yes, I believe they can be trusted for now."

Cleaning up this mess will be hard. Over the decades of protecting the Society, blood had been spilled. He hoped it didn't come to that. It wasn't like he had a hit man on retainer. He didn't even want to be on this particular retainer.

"I want to know as soon as anything changes at all. I want to know if Hedge gets sick, even a sneeze. We need to stay ahead of this thing, Mr. Andrews."

"Understood. I've gotten the boys settled down. Jim and Marie are still in Chicago, but I don't know how long I can keep them away from this. And I don't know how to convince Jim to commit."

The lawyer thought about the Andrews family drama. No one would believe that Henry Andrews would hold anyone at gunpoint. Jerry Vleet maybe. Frank York back in the day. But not Henry.

As a matter of fact, as he flipped through the thick file on his desk, the only trouble out of Henry was when Henry's wife fell ill. That was quite the mess, but it was cleaned up, nice and tidy before the lawyer had taken over the Societal reigns at his father's retirement.

"Sounds like they're too worried about each other to notice anything off in the country. Let them sort out their affairs, but keep Oliver near. The boy might be the only reason Jim comes back."

"I don't like using Oliver like that. He's not a pawn; he's my grandson. I'll keep him with me, but not as bait."

"However you see fit for now, but do give your son a reason to come back. He must be the one to inherit the land. Married or divorced."

"I'll see what I can do."

"Remember, if anything at all changes, I'll—"

"I'll be in touch." Henry hung up.

The lawyer ran his hands through this hair and leaned back in his chair again. He cursed his father and all the rest of his ancestors under his breath and spun the chair to face the family photos.

He admired the dogs, posed under the big oak in their backyard, and decided the canines might be the only ones worth the hassle.

CHAPTER 18

KNOX CHECKED the GPS for Earl's car. Still no movement. He'd tailed the rusty blue pickup for many miles to a hole-in-the-wall town where a plump kid tumbled out of the truck and sauntered into a nondescript house.

The truck then went another mile or so until it turned down a gravel lane surrounded on either side by thin clumps of trees.

He drove past the lane's end several times and decided this must be Overall's home base. The other kid, the scrawny one, never got out of the truck and had disappeared down the lane with the old man.

Knox parked his car about a half mile down the road and left a note on the windshield saying he'd run out of gas and was walking to town —just in case anyone cared to take notice. He'd seen no traffic of any sort on the old country road, so he wasn't too concerned. He'd stashed the laptop and binoculars in his duffle bag and headed for the gravel lane.

At the tree line's edge, he could make out a farmhouse, barn, and tractor through the twigs and branches. Pretty dull stuff. How did anyone survive in such conditions? He ducked behind a larger tree, sheltering out of view of the house, swatted a gnat from his neck, and refocused the binoculars.

There.

Two people—two old men—he'd not seen yet, apparently in a heated argument, arms waving, fingers pointing, on the front porch. How weary Knox was of old men…

He scanned the house through the lenses.

Some movement through an upstairs window. Probably the boy.

He knelt to a more comfortable position, ready to wait for however long for the next clue to reveal itself. He rested his elbows on a fallen tree trunk and focused on the property. Overalls finally arrived on the porch, ushering the others inside. The screen door's slam echoed down the lane and actually made Knox jump.

He'd have to remember about the door.

He had surveillance equipment in the car, but the sunlight was starting to fade and he needed to establish some sort of pattern of behavior of the farmhouse occupants to be able to get the gear in the right place. He'd never been able to get inside Earl's home. Margaret was always there unless she was in the hospital, and then Earl would unpredictably take respite behind the massive oak door of his abode.

The stick boy had come out to the porch and seemed content to stare at the fields and do nothing.

Wasted talent. Wasted mind.

Knox could mold that young man into something grand. Something powerful.

Something not weak.

Knox could tell even from this distance that weakness dripped off the boy like rot. Knox twisted next to the tree trunk, his shirt and pants damp with the evening dew. The scent of decaying leaves enveloped him as he shuffled.

The boy stood and stretched, gazing around the yard.

Then the boy stared at the tree line.

Where Knox was hiding.

His heart raced and he could hardly hold the binoculars steady in his sweaty palms. He'd not been made on a tail—ever.

Now twice in one day.

There's no way the boy could see him. He focused on the kid's face. He wasn't looking directly at Knox, but close.

Too close.

Knox slumped further behind the tree trunk and waited for an eternity.

Carefully, slowly, he edged up to peer over the log toward the porch.

The empty porch.

"Oliver, get in here."

I'd been staring to the edge of the tree line. I thought I'd seen movement, but I couldn't be sure. Probably an animal or bushes blowing. I went in the house.

"Just got off the phone with your dad. He and Marie are trying to work things out, but it's shaky. And I had to tell them about your adventure because the principal's gonna want their signatures on the discipline form. Under the circumstances, though, they'll take mine so long as I communicated to all the parents what you and Hedge did." Granddad doesn't seem mad, just burdened with the chaos.

I tear up. Again.

I don't want to bring anyone trouble, especially Granddad. With the Lamp of Death hovering over the property like a lightning bolt ready to strike, I'm beginning to understand why Granddad is so adamant that Dad take over the farm. So much has happened in a few short days. I feel like I'm not even in my body some moments. Like I'm watching myself from a screen somewhere. Like I'm in a science fiction world where someone writes the next sentence, and me, my avatar, moves stupidly along at their will.

Granddad puts an arm around me "Your parents love you, Oliver." I shrug. I *know* they do. They *say* they do. I don't *feel* they do. "And Hedge is going to be okay. We'll figure it all out." I don't know about that, either. No one is ever straight with me. Seldom does anyone ever give me the full truth.

"...chickens, and then we'll talk some more," Granddad was

relaying information, but I miss half of it wallowing in uncertainty.

I go outside and feed the chickens—the ladies are happy to see me, but only because I carry their food, not because they want me around. I toss the feed buckets aside and decide to walk to try to take my mind off the day's events.

Unlikely.

At least I could weep without anyone seeing. Weep for my friend—who's probably dying—and my parents who are moving closer and closer to divorce.

I remember the movement in the trees from before and want to check it out. Probably was nothing. Worst-case scenario, it was a wild coyote, rabid and crazed to be out before the sun set.

I hesitate, slow my pace, but then I move forward with purpose. Perhaps that coyote would put me out of my misery. Then it wouldn't be the worst-case scenario anymore.

"It" would all be over…

I'm twenty feet from the trees when Granddad calls me back to the house.

Not now.

I desperately want to be alone.

Since I've caused enough trouble for one day, I put the coyote on hold and sprint across the yard.

Granddad is hollering at me before I reach the front porch. "Hedge's mom called. He's in the ER." Granddad pulls his keys from his bibs. "We need to see if his symptoms match Margaret's."

I can't remember the last time my stomach didn't hurt. And when I think it couldn't hurt worse, another round of bad news punches me dead center.

And this is all my fault. My fault for dragging Hedge into our family's tangled mystery.

My legs barely lift me into the pickup.

On the way down the lane, I stare into the trees. I see no rabid coyote waiting to end my pain.

I see nothing at all.

It must've been my wishful thinking.

CHAPTER 19

WE ARRIVE at the ER and check in with the assistant at the front desk. Fallston doesn't have enough population to support a high-class hospital. The first floor houses the emergency room—which I'm unfortunately familiar enough with thanks to Billy and my constant battle with stomach issues. The other two floors hold enough beds for the elderly recovering from pneumonia, the occasional mother in labor, and what they called an intensive care unit, though no one is sure how intensive the care could be in such a miniscule facility.

The staff members, however, don't act like they work in a tiny hospital. They run the place like a marine base.

When Granddad asks where to find Hedge, the lady says, "There's no one here by that name." He looks confused until I clear things up.

"His real name is Walter Conrad."

She glares at me and then at Granddad over the rim of her glasses and pushes back a strand of hair into her tightly wound bun. "Still, unless you're family or you have special permission from the family…"

"Oh, good grief." Granddad is about to lose all patience. "Can't you just—" She cuts him off with a pointed finger toward the registration area.

"They can help you there and you must contact the guardian."

We finally figure out Hedge has indeed been moved to ICU and can only have one visitor at a time. And those visitors have to be over 18. Granddad throws another fit, much like the frustration I'd seen just before the shotgun came out of the corner the other day.

It works, though, and I'm permitted to see my friend. Granddad's temper, though embarrassing, causes a bit of pride to well up in my chest. Don't mess with Granddad, man. He'll come unglued. I almost smile.

Granddad stays in the waiting room with Hedge's mom while I go down the hall. I've never been in this part before. I was too young to visit Granny when she'd been on this floor…

I find Hedge's room and peek around the corner. Hedge is propped up in the bed, watching TV. He doesn't *look* all that sick, and he smiles at me.

"Hey, Ol."

"Hey." I shuffle through the doorway a few steps.

"You gonna come in or do I have to go over there?" Hedge grins. He's still a snot, so that's encouraging. But the thin line of pink that stains his teeth near his gum line is not.

"Dude, you're bleeding."

Hedge takes a swish of water and spits it into the pitcher. "Yeah. That's been happening. I only feel a little weak, but the ER doc said my blood looked bad, so they sent me up here." He nods toward the television hooked to a giant metal arm coming from the ceiling. "TV's terrible. Only ten channels. Too cheap for a dish, but, hey, did you know they have *two* elevators here? They keep the other one a secret." Hedge looks me over and pauses a minute. "You look sicker than I feel. What's going on?"

I slump in an uncomfortable recliner covered in pink vinyl in the corner of the room. I think about the huge day we'd had and the news about my parents. "Mom and Dad are not working things out, even though Granddad says they are. I could tell by his tone." I watch as Hedge hopelessly flips through all ten channels and back again. "And I'm sorry you're in here. This is my fault, too."

"Don't worry about me. Seems the higher in the hospital, the smarter the docs. And I'm on the top floor."

"This hospital only has two floors."

Hedge gives another bloody grin and shrugs. "Sorry about your parents. I hope they don't make you choose a side like mine did to me."

I hadn't even thought about that potentiality. "You had to choose?"

"Yeah. It was the hardest thing ever. But I thought Mom could use the help. Dad didn't seem to want to be around much in the first place. But now he's mad 'cause I chose Mom. I was only nine or ten, but I was more mature than he ever was. Oh well." He stops clicking the remote and looks at me. "He's on his way, you know. My dad."

"Really? How long's it been since you saw him?"

"Several years, I guess. He sends cards and junk, but never on time for birthdays or anything."

It's strange, talking to Hedge like this. We mostly gossiped about kids at school and talked video game strategy or griped about homework. But this was getting deep, and I'm not all too comfortable with it. It is nice, though, to have a friend who understands twisted families. "That's good, that he's coming."

"Yeah. One good thing coming from these bloody gums and rash on my back." Hedge leans up and tries to pull his hospital gown open for me to see.

I startle at the viney, twisted rash.

Like the one Margaret has on her arm. The mark on Hedge's neck is more pronounced than when I first spotted it at Earl's earlier today and now it's snaked its way between his shoulder blades.

"I can't see it. What's it look like? Itches like a devil's armpit."

"Yeah, it's red and blotchy and with purple lines running all through."

Hedge slumps back in the bed after rubbing the spot with the fork from his dinner tray. "Like Margaret's?"

"Sort of." I downplay it and change the subject. "You want me to bring you anything? Something to eat or anything?"

Hedge tosses the fork onto the tray. "Nah. Mom's bringing my handheld tomorrow, and I'm not allowed to eat junk here, I guess."

"So, you're a rule-follower now? After the day we've had?"

Hedge shrugs. "Guess so."

We chat for a while longer until a grumpy nurse tells me to leave and that the staff has already broken the rules to let me visit in the first place.

I fist-bump Hedge and meet Granddad at the elevator. Granddad calls to Mrs. Conrad and says for her to tell him if he can do anything at all for their family.

The elevator doors slide closed. Granddad stares at the stainless steel door. "Reminds me of your Granny."

"Hedge's mom? How so?"

"No, not her. Hedge's illness. Very…similar." Granddad wipes dampness from his eyes on the sleeve of his shirt. I was too little to remember the details. And now I'm overwhelmed with details and don't know what to say to him.

When the slowest elevator in the state of Illinois travels all of one floor and jars to a stop, something sparks deep inside me. The mature Oliver comes to the surface. The one resolved to beat all of it. Despite the tiredness, the hopelessness, and the stress. I glance at Granddad, the old man's eyes still fighting back the tears.

Before the elevator doors slide open, I know what I have to do.

I am going to destroy that cursed lamppost.

CHAPTER 20

KNOX COULDN'T BELIEVE his luck—or his magic. Whichever his ancestors would approve of. The kid had come within a few yards of finding him yesterday evening. After the pair had flown out of the gravel drive in the pickup, Knox had retrieved his surveillance gear from his car and hiked back to the farmhouse, hoping the whole time that they didn't have some rabid guard dog he didn't know about.

They didn't.

Getting in had been easy. The doors weren't locked. Knox had planted a couple of mini cameras—one in the living room and one in the kitchen. He'd done a cursory sweep of the whole place, but he found no bronze-plated items. The kid's room was neat as a pin—nothing was out of place.

A perfectionist.

He'd helped himself to an apple from the kitchen counter and a small bottle of juice from the fridge. He deserved the reward for a hard day's work, and it served as his supper.

He'd stood in the middle of the small living room. A couch. A couple of old chairs. A piano. He smiled as he ran his fingers across the ivory keys. A shiver shot through him as he thought about how close he was to having his dream. His freedom.

When he'd left the house, he'd been careful to avoid leaving evidence or footprints—except for the missing food, which he didn't think would be missed—and he'd been extra careful to not slam the screen door.

Back at the car for the night, he'd checked his laptop. Earl's dot remained still. Right there in the quiet Chicago neighborhood.

Knox had spent the night in the driver's seat. No need for a blanket; it was almost too hot to sleep.

He welcomed the predawn hours with the remembrance of yesterday's hopefully fruitful tail to the country. If nothing came of this run in a couple of days, he'd head back to the city and recalculate what the next steps would be.

In the meantime, he packed up his gear and walked to the tree line before the sun crept any higher. He assumed that Overalls and the scrawny kid had returned sometime after dark last night. He wanted to settle in behind the log before the members of the house stirred.

As the sun peeked higher in the east, the screen door slammed. It appeared Overalls and the kid were getting after the typical farm chores, then Overalls got into the truck and drove off.

Mr. Perfectionist waved to the old guy before his eyes settled on Knox's tree line again. Knox felt that uneasy quiver of being revealed —a feeling he wasn't used to and most definitely did not appreciate.

And that a weakling like Mr. Perfectionist could evoke it so easily —not once, but twice—made it all the more sour.

Knox ducked a bit lower, but kept his binoculars trained on the kid, who rounded the corner of the house and came back with a shovel and headed down the lane. This time, thought Knox, he was surely going to be caught. He dug himself into the ground as low as he could go and pulled a few loose branches over himself—not that that would do much good.

And he waited.

But nothing happened. When he ventured a look toward the lane, the kid had kept walking. Maybe he was performing another mundane farm chore. Maybe he'd buried something.

Maybe something with a bronze plate.

Knox had no choice but to follow. This may be his big chance—the difference between a life of magical misery or evil happiness.

He stood and quietly brushed the leaves and debris from his damp clothing. He held his arm across his stomach for a brief moment.

He was going to have to do something about this queasy feeling...

It was dark when we'd arrived home last night, and I had to wait until first light and after the chores to dig around in the wagon attachment we'd occasionally hitch to the tractor. Granddad was going to town, and I know I have to act fast. Before someone stops me or before I chicken out.

That's the funny things about resolutions. In the moment you decide something, something big and important, you feel ten feet tall and invincible. In the moment you're *doing* that something, you feel like a freaked-out four-year-old staring into the eyes of a rabid German shepherd.

The black wagon, or "buggy," as Granddad called it, hadn't proved as useful as he'd hoped and now we use it to keep our long-handled tools off the leaky barn floor. Other farmers in town, the ones with the newer setups, used their "buggies" in town parades, and loaded the wagons up with hay bales and little kids in overalls throwing out candy to onlookers. I stand on one of its tires and lean over the narrow edge. Post-hole diggers, rakes, hoes and shovels. I dig deep for a shovel that won't be missed and wrestle it free from the clutter.

I jog across the chicken coup yard—only a couple of the ladies bother to look up from their morning feed to acknowledge me. I think about checking in the tree line, but I don't have time to waste. Part of my punishment for the field trip incident is a two-day suspension from classes. The Oliver from last week would've died at that news. The Oliver from this week isn't the same kid.

Hedge is lying in a hospital bed because of me. My parents will likely divorce over this land—and a myriad of other reasons. I have to get to the post.

Break the light.

Dig it up.

Or something.

And I need to do it before Granddad finds out. I know what it could mean if the light flashes green again, but I have nothing to lose.

I wade through the corn, using the shovel to push the stalks away and cut down on the chance of getting sliced by the leaves. A couple of times I stop and listen. Paranoia runs deep in my gut and I have the feeling someone is watching me.

It's the scared little kid in me. Trying to flee. That flight-or-fight thing.

I walk to the clearing, sticking the end of the spade into the ground with each step. I approach the post and run a hand across the scroll work on the iron. Now or never.

I draw back the shovel and send it flying through the air in one massive whack.

Nothing. Nothing but the clang of metal on metal echoing past the clearing, into the rows of corn and beans and the scant tree lines dotting the edge of the field.

I look closely. Not a scratch.

I'm tall enough that when I raise the shovel above my head, the blade is even with the base of the glass panels surrounding the lighting element. I reach backward with the shovel and with all my might I bring the metal head zipping directly into the lamp. The force reverbs back up my arms, sending a shockwave from my wrists to my shoulders.

Nothing.

The shovel's head bounces off the light with no effect whatsoever. The bulb in the lamp didn't shatter. The post didn't wobble. None of the iron décor is marred. Not in the slightest.

Nothing.

I turn my attention to the bronze plate that had shot sparks at me and Hedge. The plate similar to the one on Earl's camera. I lift the shovel again and swing down hard. The clash of metal rings in my ears, and I am sure Granddad can hear it all the way in town.

Nothing.

No sparks. No marks.

I try digging under the post. I can't budge the muddled mess of pebble and brick at its base even with the shovel. It's as if the universe's strongest superglue has coated the whole ground and not one pebble would shift in the slightest.

I swing at the base again.

At the pole.

At the light.

Each time, the only effect is on my muscles and my pride. Lactic acid builds up in my arms and ribs. I ache all over, but I keep swinging. And shouting.

And then both.

I swing and beat and yell until the head falls off the shovel and I have nothing left but tears.

I slump to the ground, my back resting against the cold, black iron of the pole and weep. Sweat rolls from me in great drips, mixing with hot tears and snot.

I've grown so tired of weeping. For feeling sorry for myself. Feeling sorry for Mom and Dad and Hedge.

I can't do it anymore.

I have no control over this situation any more than I could control my life when Billy was a part of it. Granddad will likely find out about this episode—or maybe not. Mom and Dad will divorce—or maybe not. Hedge might live through this.

Or maybe not.

And I can't change one thing about any of it.

And I have no strength to care anymore.

Knox stared wide-eyed at the tantrum the boy had with the iron pole. From three corn rows in and off to the side, he'd watched the whole thing unfold through his binoculars. He'd been so careful not to make any noise through the gawdawful crops. Blood trickled from his face and arms where the leaves sliced into his skin. He hated the sight of his own blood. It reminded him that he was, at least in part, human.

The kid had finally given up. Nearly an hour of swinging and shouting at the post, and the metal masterpiece didn't give in. Knox could make out a slight bulge at the base of the pole that looked like a plaque. He was in a bad position to see it directly, but he believed, and hoped, that this was the object he'd been searching for. He'd have to approach it to be certain.

The post was likely the very object Earl had spent so much time and energy trying to locate. Maybe he could kill two birds with one stone. But how to steal something that clearly can't be moved or taken apart?

Knox grinned as blood continued to ooze from the corner of his mouth. He wiped it on his shirt sleeve.

Well, my dear Knox, his father's voice echoed in his mind, *you don't* steal *it. You acquire everything attached to it.*

He needed to own the land. Plain and simple. And hacking, well that was easy. Manipulating people and circumstances was firmly within his skillset, especially since most of the players he'd seen in this chapter of the story were simple country folks.

Or, it may mean getting rid of those who've already enjoyed a nice long life up to a ripe old age—or a young age…

He shook off a wave of excitement to focus on the kid. Knox still didn't understand the connection these people had with Earl, and that bothered him.

At last, the kid got up and headed into the corn the same way he'd come, shovel handle dragging behind him and the shovel head tucked under a scraggly arm. Knox smiled.

The boy had revealed more to Knox in this last hour than he'd been able to find on his own in the last few months.

Knox found Earl after hacking hospital databases for matches to physical symptoms the artifacts caused. He'd tracked Earl because he'd found a disfigured and dying Margaret. He'd found the kid because he found Earl. All he had to do now was find the owner of the land to finally find his own peace.

And the kid would help him do that, too.

He waited until he could no longer see the tops of the corn jostling with the boy's retreat. He dug out his last small, black camera and approached the light post. He could feel the electricity coming from the center of the clearing. He wondered if the kid could feel the same thing.

Probably not.

Because Knox was special. And the boy likely wasn't.

Green rays interspersed with bright blue bursts of energy shot from the lamppost, glowing brighter the closer he came. He circled the post, searching the base for the plate, already knowing what he'd find.

He bent to touch it. He brushed away the pebbles. He picked up a few pieces of broken brick and threw them aside. The bronze oozed a red welcoming glow, warm to the touch.

Knox smiled as he reached high up to the post to attach the camera to one of the decorative wheels, which was gently vibrating under his touch. The vines and flowers grew and breathed under his fingers.

He checked the angle of the camera and stepped back to take in the sight.

Fields all around. The beautiful artifact in the clearing.

He grasped the pole with both hands and leaned his face next to the metal. He experienced his next moves as if in virtual reality, complete with sight, touch, and smell. He knew exactly what to do. Each and every step to take. He knew without looking at the GPS or his surveillance maps. Warm peace spread from the pole to the top of his head down through his fingers and toes.

In that moment, he was glad he'd found Earl and the kid. He felt alive for the first time in years. Energy flowed from the artifact into his being, a life-giving force complete with crystal-clear clarity of thought and control of emotion.

At that moment, he was glad his ancestors had chosen this path for him.

He wouldn't let them down.

CHAPTER 21

MARGARET WAS WEAK, but stable for the moment. The ambulance pulled away for the second time in a week. The paramedics knew the old couple well; they also knew of the couple's wishes for Margaret to die at home in peace, but not in pain.

Earl was preparing soup, trying to take his mind off death and despair, when the call came in.

"Is this Earl?"

"Yessir, how may I help you?"

"This is Gabe from the flea market. We've met a few times before. And, well, I think I may have found something you'd be interested in."

"How's that?" The last thing Earl needed was another brass-plated object in his life. He'd almost killed a kid—maybe he *did* kill the kid— and he was no closer to helping his wife. His heart ached for young Hedge. He thought of how badly Oliver must feel for being a part of it; Earl knew that feeling all too well.

"Well, it has a plate and it's old and—"

"Out with it, son." Earl's impatience mounted. Gabe seemed to be a bit of a selfish guy, only in the hunt for money. He didn't enjoy the vintage items he came across. Probably didn't bother looking up their history or significance. Gabe had little respect for the antique business, and he was likely trying to find "that one item" that would land him a windfall of cash so he could play video games the rest of his days

"I think it's a telegraph. Don't know if it has working parts. Five hundred dollars, and it's yours."

Earl's curiosity piqued. He just couldn't turn it off after all these years of searching for an answer. This *might* be something to help and not hurt. And a telegraph fits the timeline. But did he need it? Did he want to mess around with another object?

"Too much money. Not interested." Earl stalled. He knew Gabe would price the item high after Earl had been so interested in the camera last week.

"Would you go four hundred?"

Earl though for a moment and stalled again. "I don't think my wife would be too happy with me…" The camera had only one more exposure left before he'd have to hunt the world over for more vintage supplies.

"I don't know. This bronzy plate is in better condition than the one on the camera. I think the lowest I'll go is three-fifty," Gabe countered. "What is this plate? A family heirloom or something?"

Earl was growing irritated. Gabe had asked the same question of the camera. Earl gave the same answer. "Something like that." If Gabe only knew what he held. "I'll agree to two hundred and no more."

Gabe took a moment to answer. "Well, I guess that'll have to do. No one else will want this. I think the switch may be broken. It's loose."

Earl snapped at Gabe. "You should have been upfront with me about that, young Gabe. I don't think I want it now."

"Okay, okay. I'll take one hundred dollars and you can pick it up in the morning at the flea market. Fair?"

"Fair enough." Earl hung up the phone. He was glad to have haggled Gabe down on the price—that will be his only productive accomplishment for the day.

He worried about bringing the telegraph into the house. He could leave it in his car trunk. If it turned out a fake, he'd fix the handle and

Margaret would have a new addition for her growing collection of old-time pieces.

He finished the soup and delivered it to his wife's bedside.

"Here, sweetheart. It's nice and hot. I'll help—"

Margaret held up a feeble hand and shook her head.

"You must eat, dear."

"No," she rasped. "Let me be."

"Later, then."

She shook weakly again. "No, please. Let me be. It's time to stop."

Earl had been through this with her before, and he always managed to rally her back to fight another round. To fight for them. To fight for a bit of a future, however long that would be at their ages. He loved her so much it hurt. He'd give anything—

"Help the boy. Leave me be." A single tear slid down her face, tracing the outline of the deformity as it fell.

"You rest, Love." Earl kissed her cheek. He pulled a chair close to the bed. He held her hand gently and stroked her snow-white hair until she fell into a fitful sleep. He bent to kiss her forehead now riddled with sweat from pain and the medications from the paramedics. "I love you so much," he whispered.

Earl went to the parlor and closed the bedroom door behind him. His hand lingered on the doorknob. He wondered how many more times he'd open that door to find Margaret still breathing. Still on this side of eternity. He wondered which time he'd open it to find that Margaret had left him.

Left him alone and broken.

And him having failed to be the knight in shining armor she once thought him to be.

His old red chair was a welcome sight. An old friend. How many hours had he spent there planning, hoping, and dreaming? He slid down onto the worn cushion, opened the side table drawer, and removed the photo of Hedge.

He wasn't about to give up. Not now.

The telegraph held a glimmer of hope. If Margaret didn't make it, he may be able to help the boy.

She had given him permission to do so.

Leave me be.

The words echoed in his soul. He couldn't leave her be. He loved her too much.

Tomorrow is another day. Another chance.

He leaned forward, knobby elbows resting on aching knees, head in hands.

And wept.

CHAPTER 22

WEDNESDAY BROUGHT sunshine and welcome warmth for Earl who'd been chilling despite the June night. Probably stress.

He'd gotten up as early as he could and called the home nurse he'd hired years ago for Margaret. The nurse was good with his wife, but she always gave Earl dirty looks like how dare he leave his wife in her condition. It couldn't be helped, and Earl had grown used to it over the years.

All of the flea markets and "treasure hunts" were *for* his wife. How could he ever explain that? He also knew to leave whatever he might have purchased in the trunk lest the judgmental nurse give him a second round of dirty looks when he returned home.

Gabe was setting up his tent and tables in the usual spot and recognized Earl right away. The vest and the cane gave him away. He always tried to dress like a gentleman. And, Earl likely held the only cash Gabe would make all day.

"Got it right here, Mr. Earl."

"Let's have a look-see." Earl handled the telegraph in much the same way he'd approached the camera last week. He turned it over, inspected all the parts. The switch wasn't broken after all. Gabe had no clue what he was doing, but Earl didn't have the time to dawdle with him about it. The bronze plate was similar to the camera's, but slightly less aged.

He handed Gabe another hundred dollar bill.

Gabe grinned and held the bill up to the sun. "You know, I had the bank check the other one, and they said it was real. And old. These bills are probably older than anything I've got for sale."

"Probably," nodded Earl. He'd had some of those bills since before he and Margaret were married.

They were going to see Paris with those bills.

They were going to buy their first child a motorized car with those bills.

They were…

"Have a good day. I'll keep looking for stuff like this, if you want." Gabe packed the telegraph in a cardboard box for Earl.

"This'll do, Gabe. This'll do." Earl headed back to his car, box under one arm, cane in the other hand. The lid of the box flapped in the breeze and he caught sight of something he'd missed on his first inspection of the piece. This plate was smoother, more defined.

He put the opened box in the trunk of his car. Earl ran his finger over the marking at the bottom of the plate. His heart sank and his already weak knees felt paper-thin. His cane dropped to the grassy lot, and he leaned against the edge of the bumper, frozen.

There, when the light caught the metal just so, etched in bronze was a decoration embedded behind the wording.

And it was identical to the marks on Margaret's arm.

The news of the telegraph brightened Margaret. Earl hadn't seen her this alert, this willing to sit up and make conversation, in a very long time. Her voice was weak, but she had a spark of life in her eyes that Earl longed for.

"We should call that nice gentleman and let him know about it. Better yet," she rasped, "we should take this and the camera to them. It's been a long time since I've been anywhere."

Earl looked at her, dumbfounded. "Darling, you're too weak, Even when you weren't bed-ridden, you never wanted to leave the house. You—"

"It's high time I got over myself and did something for someone else. You've been globetrotting, scooping up whatever you could find to help me. Now it's my turn to help those poor boys." Margaret crossed her arms.

That was it then. He'd seen *that* gesture before, but it was ages ago. And no use arguing with her when she crossed her arms. No use stalling or trying to put her off, either.

Earl's smile broke through the stale gloom of the bedroom.

Decision made.

"Well, I guess I'll gas up the car and pack up the trunk and we'll take a trip." Bounding strength replaced the pain and weakness in his knees. "Stay put now, until I can help you. Be thinking about what you want to wear." Earl winked at his wife.

Despite the disfigurement, she was beautiful. Beautiful spirit, beautiful smile. She was his breath.

He watched her raise a hand to her good side, then reach to feel the side of her face that had forced her behind walls for so many years.

People were so cruel.

Earl and Margaret had tried to make a life for themselves, but the name-calling and mocking were too much for her sweet spirit to endure. Several times the bullying escalated to vandalism and physical threats. The last time she'd ventured out of the house was to go to the market. Earl had accompanied her, like a gentleman should. Some thugs had waited for her behind a dumpster with raw eggs and rotten tomatoes at the ready.

And the food hadn't been simply tossed; they'd hurled it with such force that he and Margaret had come home with bruises on their necks and arms.

"No more. I won't do this to you anymore. I'll stay home," she had said after the attack. She was only twenty-one. Her blond hair was matted to her face with egg yolk despite the flow of tears trying to wash it away.

Now, fifty years later, she's ready to leave the house to help someone else who may be in the same danger.

She still had that wonderful spirit he fell in love with five decades ago. He'd wondered countless times what his life would have been like if they hadn't snapped that last photo at their wedding.

If those bronze plates hadn't sparked out on the street that day.

He pulled the suitcase from the hall closet and almost laughed. They'd purchased the luggage together, right before the wedding. They were going to travel the world. This was prime, vintage luggage. Never used and over fifty years old. It would fetch a pretty penny today. Gabe probably wouldn't have a clue of its value if he came across anything like this set. He ran his hands across the brown leather. This one had no wheels like the modern-day baggage has. This was a gentleman's suitcase, made for a man to carry for his wife.

He brought the case into the bedroom where Margaret was working on sitting up, her legs dangling over the side of the bed. She wobbled and struggled to sit straight, but she had more energy and enthusiasm since he'd shown her the telegraph than she'd had in the last twenty years.

"Here, dear. Let me help you."

"I want to get going. I want to get there before night. How long do you think?"

Earl tugged at his vest. "Three hours if we drive straight through." He didn't think they should—he didn't think he could go that far at once on his own, for that matter.

"Oh." The same realization hit Margaret. "Go halfway and then the rest tomorrow? Maybe we get a room?" And this time, she winked at him.

Earl's eyes widened and he stroked his beard a little more nervously. "Oh dear. Let's take one thing at a time, shall we?" Earl's heart soared. He was ready to try his old knees at skipping. He helped her dress in street clothes. Clothes that hadn't seen the light of day for quite some time.

After quite a bit of effort, Margaret sat up in her wheelchair. He would get her to the top of the steps before she'd have to walk. He had her wait in the parlor while he loaded the trunk with the camera and telegraph—each carefully wrapped in blankets to keep the two bronze plates far from one another. The suitcase went in last. He slammed the trunk shut and faced the house. He could see his wife watching him from the window, the white curtains framing her frail figure.

She looked so peaceful. So alive.

A half hour later, he managed to load her and the folded wheelchair into the car. They held hands as Earl pulled away from their little home —together—for the first time in a half century.

Neither aware of the blinking red light under the back bumper.

CHAPTER 23

YESTERDAY, I pouted and rested and recovered from my meltdown at the lamppost. Or tried to. And I visited Hedge. Today I went back to school, tail tucked between my legs, tried to avoid the stares and jeers, and managed to survive the mundane routine of class-work until I could get Granddad to take me back to the intensive care unit.

I step off the bus at the end of our lane. The sky had burst open as we loaded up after school and the rain hadn't stopped. By the time I reach the front porch, I'm soaked through.

I toss on some dry clothes and dig the phone out of my backpack. No missed calls.

No surprise.

Dad called the last couple of mornings to lie about how well everything is going. Mom's only called once.

Each day it becomes a little harder for Hedge to track with conversation or to make his usual dumb jokes. I feel terrible about it, but all I can do now is be there for him.

I knock on Granddad's bedroom door and speak through it. "Can I get a ride to the hospital? I wouldn't bother you, but it's raining, and—"

"Not today. Not right now anyway." Granddad opens his door, dressed in a business suit and tie that makes him look nothing like a farmer. "Put something decent on. We've got a viewing to go to." Granddad has the same expression as when he'd seen Margaret.

"What?" My head spins even though I should be getting used to bad news. Or at least numb to it.

"Eddie." Eddie the farmer—Granddad's friend. Eddie from when Granddad called the meeting with the landowners. He was in our living room less than a week ago.

"What happened?"

"His daughter said he had a heart attack. Happened yesterday while he was in the field." He looked straight into my eyes as if I had something to do with it.

I take a step back. "Do you think he was at the post—"

"No, I think he was tending his field. He was found slumped over inside the tractor, much too far away for the light post to be the cause. I think he was old. I think he was stressed." As he speaks, I can tell he doesn't believe a word of what's coming out of his own mouth.

Granddad straightens his tie, jerks the tie completely off, then redoes the whole thing. "The last time I wore this dumb thing was at Frank's funeral. The time before that was at your..." He trails off.

Granny.

Granddad recovers from the memory. "Get dressed. No jeans. No nasty t-shirt, please."

I nod. I'll call Hedge's mom and let her know that I would be late or unable to come this evening. Mrs. Conrad had begun to seem grateful for my visits; those times gave her a chance to stretch her legs or go home to shower while I watched over Hedge and fetched water or the remote. Or just sat.

It also gave her a chance to get away from Mr. Conrad.

I pull off my tee and replace it with the collared shirt Mom bought me for picture day at school. I search through the back of my closet to find dress pants—pants an inch too short and tight around the middle, but they'll have to do.

My "good" shoes were a size too small and hurt my feet.

Every time I turn around, I'm reminded of how nothing is in my control—even something as stupid as pants and shoes.

We get into the pickup and head to town. Neither of us speak.

I know Granddad is—was—close to Eddie. They had been best friends for as long as I knew. Like how close Hedge and I are. Unexpectedly and without my permission, my brain plays out Hedge's funeral. I see my best friend lying in the casket, his mom and dad weeping in the corner. I can smell the cut flower arrangements and stale cookies the well-meaning church ladies would have baked two days prior…

My gut knots up tight and I try to shake off the thought. Back to the present nightmare. At least for the moment. Granddad was speaking "…put together in a hurry. The service will be simple. Immediate family only for the burial."

I listen as he goes on about Eddie's plans. I trace the glass with my finger as water droplets snake and slide in hapless patterns on the window until we pull into the lot.

The funeral home is crowded. It doesn't help that the facility is small, but Fallston doesn't have a big anything. We find a place to park and dart inside out of the rain, now coming down much harder. I'm brushing off water from my too-long hair when I spot my parents in the corner of the entryway.

Both of them.

Together.

And Billy is standing with them.

I look at Granddad who, by his jaw drop and raised brows, didn't know they'd be coming either.

"Dad! Mom!" I rush to them and try to appear unconcerned with Billy's presence. I suddenly remember someone's died and that I shouldn't appear happy in a funeral home.

We give quick embraces. "Eddie's daughter called us. She thought we'd like to know," Mom says.

"We're leaving once the service is over, though." Dad shuffles and gazes toward the door. "Still working things out, you know." He hangs his head and turns away from Mom.

"Oh." My enthusiasm from mere seconds before deflates. "Why's Billy here?" I whisper to Dad.

"I have no idea. He got here before we did. Made your mom's day, though."

I bet it did. I step back and watch Billy interact with Mom. They always had a special bond, even after all the terrible things Billy had done to me. Both of us her sons, but one clear favorite who could do no wrong.

Billy walks toward me and bumps me hard across the shoulder, which is still sore from swinging the shovel a couple of days ago. "Moron."

I ignore him, at least outwardly, and move to sit with Dad and Granddad near the front. Granddad had been talking to Jerry, the grumpy Deep Throat farmer who'd caught me and Hedge in the field.

Two old farmers left, now. No doubt they're discussing what to do about the land. I know there is too much for two families to handle with four large farms, especially since it looks like Dad isn't interested in any of it. And especially since these are not ordinary farms.

I don't care though. I'd decided at the post when the shovel broke in two that I'd given up caring. I love Granddad, but there is absolutely nothing I can do now but behave myself.

The service drones on, and I long to be at the hospital. I focus on the bright flowers lining the casket and arranged all along the walls in those cardboard vases that they'll throw on top of the grave later. The yellows and oranges and whites of the petals are a stark contrast to the gray dead man. I shiver.

I glance over to see Billy gawking out the window. He didn't have the respect to face forward for the eulogy.

The preacher finally says "Amen" and everyone stands for a second round of courtesy hugs and handshakes, pouring attention over the family members who stand guard over poor Eddie. I find the rest of my family.

Billy makes his condolences and shoots for the door. Mom is clearly upset that Billy hadn't bothered to say goodbye to her; my goodbye hug is second rate, at best.

Dad tells me goodbye and says he probably won't call tonight since we've already seen each other. And to stay out of trouble. He gives me a light scolding for playing hooky from the field trip. And an "End the year strong, Son" pep talk.

And then he and Mom leave. Again.

Granddad sits with Jerry in deep conversation. I sit in the back row and wait. Until I can't sit any longer.

I finally nudge Granddad's shoulder. Jerry glares at me, but I ignore him.

"I'm gonna walk over to the hospital. It's not raining so hard now."

"That's fine. I'll pick you up later," Granddad's words are quick and short. But then he grabs my arm and adds, "Tell Hedge I said hi."

I nod and leave through the back door, catching sight of Billy's Volkswagen in the parking lot. I hope he doesn't follow me to the hospital. Through the rain and the foggy car windows, though, it looks like Billy has company in the passenger's seat.

A man dressed all in black, as best I can tell.

Probably a drug dealer.

CHAPTER 24

BILLY HAD SPOTTED Pale Face during the funeral of Granddad's old buddy.

Billy had only come to the Podunk town because he'd crushed on Eddie's youngest daughter years ago. But, alas, she'd gotten married, and along with the crying and weight she'd put on, he'd quickly realized he'd wasted a trip.

If Billy were honest with himself, he'd also come out of morbid curiosity regarding Oliver and Granddad. To see if Oliver had been nailed to the wall yet.

He hadn't. That brat could get away with murder.

He'd drifted his focus outside the window during the service and there was the same weird guy that had been outside that old man's house in Chicago the day Oliver ditched school.

Billy hurried through the receiving line and snuck outside to find the strange character leaning under the side awning of the funeral home. "Hey! I know you."

The guy motioned for Billy to stop yelling.

"Open your car." Billy unlocked his Volkswagen and let the guy in. He must have recognized Billy's car from the other day, too. Maybe Pale Face was tailing him. Maybe he *was* undercover police.

"What are you doing here? Who are you?" A small voice inside his head told Billy this was a bad idea. Letting a perfect stranger into his vehicle. Especially someone like this dude. But Billy ignored it. He didn't take orders from small voices.

"I could ask the same of you. You go first." Pale Face prodded.

"Not likely. Unless you got a badge, dude, you're on my turf now."

Pale Face wiped condensation from the window and watched the raindrops trickle down the glass. "Name's Knox."

"Name's Billy." Billy didn't take his eyes of the stranger.

Pale Face turned, and they sized each other up as if deciding friend or foe. Trust or don't.

Billy nodded toward the funeral home doors. "Did you know Eddie?"

"Briefly." Pale Face—Knox—grinned. Not a glad-to-know-you grin, but much more sinister than that. "Did *you* know Eddie?"

Billy nodded. "Granddad's old friend. They'd been neighbors for eternity. His daughter was a looker back in the day."

Knox raised an eyebrow. "Oh, yeah?" Knox looked out the window again. "Your Granddad have that kid with him all the time?"

"Oliver. My stupid brother—*half-brother*. Ruined my life and split our family. I'm living in Chicago because of that brat. Barely getting by." Billy couldn't stop the eruption of information.

Knox looked around the interior of the messy car. "I can see that. I've, um, ran into Oliver and his friend. You say he's a problem child?"

"Yeah, the worse kind. Goody-two-shoes, family splitter." Billy ran through in his mind what his life could have been like as an only child. If Mom hadn't needed a man to take care of her. If she could've only stood on her own two feet, like Billy's been doing for years, Oliver wouldn't exist.

Several moments passed in silence before Knox spoke. Rain tinkled against the metal of the Volkswagens roof and raindrops raced and wormed down the glass.

"Work for me. I can give you some cash, help you out a little bit." Knox paused and picked at his fingernails. "Oliver is in my way. I need him to stop running all over and stay in one place. Preferably at the farmhouse." Billy felt Knox reading him. Something about the man's eyes… "No, strike that. Preferably at the hospital."

Movement outside caught Billy's attention.

Oliver. The kid was looking in their direction like a pompous know-it-all.

Anything to make that brat's life difficult, no matter the reason, rang a sweet tune in Billy's head.

"Hospital it is. How much we talkin'?"

Knox grinned, and Billy joined him.

CHAPTER 25

"EDDIE'S DEAD."

"I heard. Jerry called me. This is unfortunate." The lawyer took the call during his family's special weekend luncheon. His wife glared at him over the pot roast when the phone vibrated on the table. He had breached one of her blasted cardinal rules of etiquette. No phones on the table. No phones during the kids' homework. No feet on the coffee table. No…No…No…

But he was glad for the disruption. "Are there any developments?"

"No, not that I'm aware of. My son showed up at the funeral, but we didn't have a chance to talk about the land before he bolted with Marie. He's still dealing with her."

"Eddie's will stipulates that his family will inherit. Does Eddie's family know the details? Of what will be required?"

"I hope so. Jim and Marie reacted badly to the whole deal—"

"Well, the shotgun didn't help, Henry. I'd like you present for the reading of Eddie's will. Your son, too. Hearing the will along with Eddie's kids—kids he grew up with—and from a lawyer might help Jim understand you're not the bad guy. This is do-or-die time for your families."

This is do-or-die time for mine, too.

"I don't know if I can get Jim to come."

"You have to. If he won't, then I'll have to call a meeting."

Hesitation on the line. "That's not necessary. A Society meeting takes too much—"

"I don't want to, but if the upcoming generations of farm heirs cause a problem with the inheritance, then I must insist on a meeting." The lawyer rubbed his brow and glanced toward the dining room. The pot roast hadn't moved. Neither had his wife. "Look, try to get everyone here for the reading and hope for the best. We need to appoint a new Head Protector, possibly two, to cover the ground you've lost this last week. I won't call a Society meeting unless the will reading goes south."

"Fair enough. I'll keep you informed."

The lawyer tried to be human once more. "Hey, how's your grandson's friend, by the way?"

"Not good and getting worse by the day. Oliver is visiting him now. "

"Well, for all our sakes, I wish him the best." The lawyer lied—so much for being human. It might be better if the kid died. They could spin the story. He'd done it a dozen times; his father and grandfather had spun stories throughout their entire careers.

If the kid lived, it would be another mouth—or two or twelve—to keep quiet about the artifacts.

And keeping people quiet was a beastly endeavor.

CHAPTER 26

BILLY WAS NEARLY GIDDY. Getting paid to be mean to the one who ruined his existence.

Not just mean—downright awful.

Billy didn't think twice about the offer. He didn't need to. Oliver was the reason he had to move out on his own so soon. Billy's real dad was who knows where, and Jim never bothered to be kind to him—let alone treat him like a son.

Oliver had walked in the direction of the hospital, so after his impromptu meeting with Knox, he'd driven his pathetic Bug to the ER parking lot and waited for Oliver to come out. Not long after, Granddad showed up, so Billy couldn't do anything right after the funeral. Too risky.

The farmhouse would be a better idea, but he needed an excuse to be there. Granddad had told Billy long ago he wasn't welcome there anymore. Everyone was always sticking up for Oliver. A few hard pushes and a couple of black eyes shouldn't have been the end of the world. It may have toughened the kid up a little.

He waited until he saw Granddad and Oliver leave the hospital before starting his engine. As Billy drove the short distance out of the 'ville and toward the farm, he formulated his excuse as music blared from the radio. He drummed his fingers on the steering wheel.

Giddy.

He pulled into the lane and Granddad wasn't too long behind him. Oliver jumped out of the pickup, glanced at Billy and went into the house. The little idiot's eyes were red and his cheeks were wet.

And Billy had done nothing to him. Yet.

"What business do you have here, Billy?"

"Uh, Mom said there was some stuff of mine in the basement that I should get before she moves out."

"Oh really? What else did she say?" Granddad raised one eyebrow.

"Nothing. Just to come and get my junk."

Granddad studied Billy for a moment then pointed at the house. "Well, get on with it then." He turned for the barn. Probably to tinker with some piece of farm stupidity. This was perfect.

Billy went into the house, but he didn't go to the basement. He scaled the stairs, three at a time, up to Oliver's room and threw open the door. Oliver was curled on the bed, crying like a sissy.

"Get out!"

"Nah. I came all this way to see you, little brother. What seems to be the trouble?" Billy said in his calmest, most reassuring tone as he took a couple steps closer to the bed.

"Get out." Oliver jumped up and rushed at Billy, arms out as if to shove him from the bedroom. Billy's adrenaline rose. Another perfect move.

Billy grabbed Oliver's outstretched arm, twisted it hard behind his back, forcing Oliver to face the opposite direction. He guided Oliver toward the stairs. Oliver was at Billy's mercy. The pair awkwardly descended the steps, Billy yanking hard on the twisted arm to keep Oliver on his feet.

They stumbled into the piano bench at the base of the steps then out the screen door, which double slammed behind the half-brothers.

"Let me go!" Oliver yelled, hoping Granddad would hear, Billy guessed.

"Nah. Like I said, we've got some catching up to do. Stop squirming, you'll hurt yourself."

Billy tried to open the door of the Volkswagen but Oliver's resistance made it difficult. He momentarily loosened his grip and Oliver broke free.

Billy swung open the car door, then lunged for Oliver, tackling him in the yard. Oliver screamed again, and Billy placed a tight hand over his mouth while twisting his opposite arm around the kid's back, lifting Oliver to his feet.

A gun shot ripped through the yard and echoed behind them into the tree line.

And then another.

Billy's grip tightened as he tried to take another step.

The third shot was close. Rocks sprang up and pinged against the blue paint of Billy's car.

"Get off my property now." Granddad aimed the shotgun straight at Billy's head.

Billy worked his way toward the back of the car, dragging Oliver along.

"Fine Gramps. Whatever you say." Billy raised his free hand in surrender, and with the other, he gave one final twist. Oliver's arm gave a satisfying pop and the kid fell to the ground behind the Bug in agony, cupping his shoulder.

Granddad took a step closer, gun at the ready. Billy dashed into the driver's side seat, started the car and put it in reverse, fully prepared to back over Oliver as he fled the down the lane.

Granddad lowered the shotgun. "Oliver, move! Roll!"

Oliver barely rolled out of the way as Billy peeled down the lane, spraying Oliver and Granddad with gravel projectiles.

Billy reached the country road and drove further into the country. He pulled over to the ditch and caught his breath. That puke of an old man nearly blew his head off.

At any rate, the only place Oliver would be going tonight was back to the hospital. Knox would be pleased.

He couldn't wait to see the satisfied smirk on old Pale Face.

CHAPTER 27

THE GPS signal beeped then beeped again, pulling Knox out of a fitful sleep. He brushed away the cobwebs and tried to straighten his neck. He'd been living in his car for the past few days.

In the middle of nowhere.

Country as far as you could see for miles in either direction. No one had stumbled on him nestled in his hideout. No farm equipment or pickups or passerby. Such a change from the city.

He set the volume on the GPS alarm as loud as possible so he could focus attention on the camera feed from the post—which he'd checked obsessively every hour around the clock since he'd planted the camera in the field. The cameras Knox had planted in the house proved more difficult. Bad signals out here in the smothering isolation. Not enough towers or satellite coverage to boost the reception. And the audio was barely audible. Too much noise from the old central air unit in the house, Knox suspected.

The GPS showed Earl was on the move. And then he'd stopped. He was somewhere halfway between Chicago and Fallston. Margaret may have died and Earl was making arrangements. For as long as Knox had watched the couple, she'd never left the house and Earl had never been away for more than a few hours at a time. Now, Earl's vehicle had been on a slow move from Chicago south toward Knox's location since Wednesday.

He checked the post and its surroundings on his screen and returned the seat upright. Billy was supposed to be here any moment. He supposed that's why the surveillance hadn't shown new activity at the post. Due to some unfortunate "accident" neither Overalls nor the kid could visit the clearing. Perhaps no one else knew what was on the property except for the owners. And now that Eddie was gone, there were just two more…

He swore under his breath about the misfortune of the failed surveillance in the house. On the other hand, to keep an eye on another set of feeds would require another person's help.

Knox fumbled in the backseat for the cash he'd promised Billy in return for incapacitating Oliver. He hated working with cash. He preferred all things electronic. But blasted Billy didn't have a bank account.

You can't tell digital lies to people who aren't digital. Knox was a master hacker and could cover his trails well. He never *paid* for anything. For most people, appearance of paying was enough. Ones and zeros in binary code signaling a computer to fool a well-meaning cashier or teller.

He was a ghost. Ghosts don't need cash. The car he sat in was a gift of his own generous system. Swiping a little plastic card for Knox was like, well, magic.

The magic had blessed him with genius and granted him access to this century where he could be most useful. Where he could be in charge of his own destiny.

He saw the crumbling blue Bug approach and Billy got out with a dumb grin.

"How'd it go?" Knox asked as he stepped into the humidity. The rain from earlier hadn't cooled anything off. Sticky, hot air fell around them like a wet blanket.

"Perfect. The stars aligned and everything went great. He's surely at the ER with a broken arm about now." Billy nodded in self approval.

"Arm? *Arm?*" He can still *walk*?" Knox felt heat rising in his spine.

"Yeah. You said keep him out of the way. You said—" Billy stopped talking when Knox got in his face.

"He can still *walk?* You fool! I need him out of the way for good."

Billy took a step back. Confusion raced across his face. "I still get paid, though, right? Granddad shot at me, for crying out loud!"

Knox pulled half the cash out of the envelope and put it in the backseat of his car. He tossed the envelope with the other half of the money to the ground with such force that the bills spilled out around Billy's feet, slowly soaking up the remnants of the rain showers.

"Next time, if there is a next time, I want you to do exactly as I say. Or you'll be the one in need of a doctor." Knox returned to his car, slammed the door and sped away as he watched Billy through the rearview mirror, standing on the side of the road like a moron with money flapping at his feet.

Heat rushed into Knox's face. He gripped the wheel until his knuckles ached. Oliver can still walk, which means he can still get in the way. Overalls is probably out for Billy's blood and will also be in the way—even more than before. Billy had made a mess of things.

This irresponsibility was probably why Billy was on the outs with his family in the first place. Knox should have known better.

He took three deep, calming breaths and felt the blood return to its rightful place and flow.

Computers never let you down. They may glitch, but you have total control over them.

Magic never lets you down. It can glitch, as well, but again, the magic can be harnessed with time and patience.

People. People are dumb and unpredictable.

He slowed the car to a more reasonable speed, one that wouldn't draw attention and breathed deeply again.

He could see it now. Billy was too old to mold into anything useful. He needed help from someone he could instill his beliefs into. He needed an assistant. All of his ancestors had assistants. And all of those assistants were young and pliable.

And, when and if the circumstances called for it—or the magic demanded it—those assistants had happy little accidents.

This current mess has too many moving parts. He had to watch the post, watch Earl's journey, and keep an eye out for artifacts. His plan wouldn't work unless he had all the pieces. All the pieces of magic paired with all his techno genius.

He felt a chill despite the swelter. He couldn't wait to set the plan in motion. All those brainless masses. All those who hurt him. He was going to end the suffering...

But he needed a second person, and Billy clearly wasn't the one. No brain power in that one.

No. He needed a trusting, young soul. Someone still young enough to believe in magic. Like Knox had been to his father so many years ago. Like his father had been to his grandfather before that. Someone young enough to entrust with real magic—but not too young to go running to Mommy.

Confidence rose to a grin on his blanched face. He knew who he needed. He entered the address for the hospital into his GPS and blasted the air conditioning.

He needed Oliver.

CHAPTER 28

I AM thankful the ER isn't busy tonight. I'm still shaking from the encounter with Billy, and Granddad is beside himself with a rage that unsettles me more than the gunfire has.

Granddad would have taken Billy out if he'd had a clear shot, I'm sure of it. The new bruises and welts Billy dealt me cover my left arm from the wrist all the way up to the elbow. By the time the nurse comes to get me, I'm unable to move my arm and my fingers are starting to go numb.

Granddad steps outside to call Mom and Dad. Dad would be enraged, but Mom would probably side with Billy, saying I'd surely done *something* to make him mad. No one would believe what happened, though. The nurse eyes Granddad with suspicion and asks me over and over who did this to me. Finally satisfied, she gives me a shot in the hip for the pain and takes me for an X-ray.

We wait in the exam room for the doctor's report. I lie on the gurney. Granddad slumps in a metal chair with his eyes closed. He'd lost his best friend, his son was AWOL, and now this. He'd pulled a gun on family for the second time in less than a week.

"You okay, Granddad?" I try to break the thick silence.

Granddad straightens in his chair and smiles sleepily. "Look at you, worried about me. I'm fine. Is there anything I can do for you?"

I shake my head and cradle my arm. The pain medication is making me sleepy, but I'm too amped up to allow rest to come. "Can we see Hedge before we leave."

"If you want, I can go upstairs to check on him for you."

"I'd like to see him, but visiting hours are done." It's been a long day and the sun had set during our drive to the hospital.

Granddad grins. "Oh, don't worry about that. We'll get around the visiting hours one way or another. Those ratchety nurses don't scare me."

I grin back and imagine Granddad showing up in the ICU with his shotgun, demanding extended visiting times. I try to keep my eyes open, but it's becoming more difficult by the minute.

The doctor comes, followed by two nurses with pitiful expressions.

"Well, what's the verdict?" Granddad asks.

"Good news and bad news. Good news—nothing's broken."

"Bad news?" I mumble. I'm losing control of my articulation.

"Your shoulder's dislocated and this is gonna hurt." The doctor and nurses approach the bed and reach for my bad arm.

Another surge of adrenaline overrides the lethargy.

I instinctively scoot to the head of the gurney in retreat. Granddad stands to get out of the way.

They lay their hands on me, pinning me to the bed.

"One, two, three…"

Then everything goes black.

When I come to, I can wiggle my fingers, but my shoulder is on fire. I'm grateful I passed out as they'd yanked my arm back into place. "Hey, there sleepyhead." Granddad is at my side.

"Hey." My head feels a bit clearer, but I'm exhausted. The stress of the past week hangs over my head and I want to see Hedge. Heck, what I really want is a bed next to Hedge upstairs so we can commiserate and sleep as much as we want.

"I've seen Hedge. He'd like a short visit tonight if you're up to it."

I brighten a bit. "Yeah, I'm up to it." Granddad had already signed the papers for the ER. A grumpy nurse puts me in a wheelchair, as I'm still unsteady from the drugs, and wheels me to the elevator.

Hedge's room is dark except for a nightlight shining from below the bed. There's not even a glow from the TV or a video game screen.

Granddad wheels me next to Hedge's bed and leaves us alone. Hedge is snoring, so I wait a few minutes before I nudge him alert. I feel guilty for interrupting his rest, but I want to talk to him.

Hedge groans at my touch and opens his eyes. I bring my right hand over my mouth to stifle a yelp. Hedge's eyes are completely red. Like every vessel had burst bright red blood into the whites.

"Wicked, isn't it?" Hedge half-grins. The way Margaret half-grinned.

"Nah. No more than when I beat you at Call of Duty." I tease, trying to lighten my own shock more than anything else.

"Docs don't know what to do with me. They may transfer me to another hospital up in Chicago if this doesn't clear, but the docs up there say they've never heard of anything like this and maybe I shouldn't be moved. My parents are real upset. Mom's been sleeping in the waiting room the whole time I've been here." Hedge's voice is weak and shaky. His mouth doesn't move symmetrically, like one side of his face is out on strike. He looks at me closer. "Hey, why are you in that chair?"

"Billy happened." I don't want to burden Hedge. I'd planned on telling him every detail, but not now. Hedge has his own dire battle. I'll have to suck it up and carry my own troubles.

"Huh. I never liked him. Even before I met him." Hedge repositions himself in the bed. "You know what?"

"What?"

"I never want Jell-O again. I never want to sleep on a plastic mattress again. I'm sick of ice chips and chicken broth. Sick of being poked and prodded. And," Hedge smiles a bloody grin, "Nurse Angela Y. is the *best* at sponge baths."

I laugh out loud. "Well, next time, I'll be sure to let Billy give me a real beating and then I'll request Angela."

"Make sure it's with a 'Y'. 'Cause Nurse Evil downstairs in the ER is 'Angela W.' See. Attention to detail." Hedge points to his temple and nods.

We both laugh until it hurts—which didn't take too long for either of us. We quiet down and the night nurse taps on the door. Our time is up.

"Well, I'll see you soon. Hopefully tomorrow, K, Hedge?"

"Okay. And Oliver?"

"Yeah."

"Whatever happens, this isn't your fault. Okay?"

The knot in my throat almost chokes off my voice. "Okay." Hedge is being gallant. I know it's my fault, and Hedge does too. Hedge is going to die. I want to scream. The pain moves from my arm to my whole being.

Agonizing pain for my dying friend.

CHAPTER 29

I TRY to avoid taking the pain medication. I'm truly spooked, afraid Billy is waiting for me around every corner. Afraid to close my eyes in some drugged stupor. Afraid to dream of Hedge and lights and death and gunfire. The medication helps my arm, but it also guarantees I'll fall asleep.

School is out of the question. I have a note that says so. I'm sickened at the thought of how many end-of-year exams I'll have to catch up on between the suspension and now this, but then I realize that at least I *can* catch up on it. Hedge may never…

It's early. The morning isn't sweltering yet, but the bugs stir already. The sun peeks over the east field. Over the scene of all the crimes…

I pull my gaze back to the front porch.

Granddad won't let me do anything around the farm to help, not haul chicken feed with my good arm or even spray their water trough out with the garden hose. I cradle my left arm, which rests fitfully in a pale blue flimsy sling. "And it better stay on for two weeks," the mean nurse had wagged her finger in my face while giving Granddad looks of contempt.

So all I can do was to sit on the porch and watch the lane. I swat the occasional gnat with my right hand, and that simple movement jars my shoulder, so I mostly leave the gnats to their business. I scan the tree line for signs of movement.

And I wait.

I wait for Billy's Volkswagen. Wait for Dad's car to come up the drive. Wait for Dad to call and tell me Mom is done with all of us. Wait for Mrs. Conrad to show up, enraged that her son has died.

I am waiting for more bad news.

I hear someone drive up the lane before I see the car. The sound of gravel under tires and the pull of an engine. My palms go wet, and I make my way closer to the front door. In case it's Billy. In case I have to hide.

But it isn't Billy. It's Earl.

I yell for Granddad as I fly off the edge of the porch, regretting this decision. I land on both feet, but I may as well have landed on my bum shoulder. I take a couple of deep breaths to clear the pain fog and run to greet Earl.

"Wow! What are you doing here?"

"Well, my young Oliver, my wife wanted to take a road trip and this was the only place she'd let me bring her." Earl grins. He rubs his eyes as he steps out of the sedan. I think he's aged ten years since we first met four days ago.

I glance across to the passenger's side where the window is rolled down. The seat has been reclined all the way back, and Margaret lifts her frail hand and waves. She gives me her best half-smile and closes her eyes.

"She's had a hard trip. We had to stop on the way last night to rest. I'm afraid I'll need some help but," he gives a slight nod toward my sling, "I'm not sure you can manage."

"Hello, there." Granddad comes around the corner. "What brings this pleasant surprise?"

"Well, we were wondering if—"

Margaret interrupts her husband. Her raspy voice is nearly swallowed by the humidity. "Could we stay here for a bit? I'd like to get to know the boys better and, and—"

"And we've found something else. Something that might help." Earl points to the trunk, and I go to the back of the car.

Granddad stops me. "Oh, no you don't. Not till I see what it is. Let's get these good people in where it's cooler and give them something to drink. Oliver, you get the drinks, I'll do the heavy lifting. And put clean sheets on your mom and dad's bed, if it won't hurt too much." Granddad turns to help Earl ready the wheelchair.

No use arguing. No use trying to prove I'm worth my weight in the middle of the driveway. I head to the kitchen to pour lemonade and rummage through the cabinets for a snack. We need a trip to the store. Since Mom and Dad had gone, the groceries are running low. No one has an appetite…

Twenty minutes pass before the old folks settle into the living room. I'm not sure how Margaret can navigate the stairs to Mom and Dad's room. "She could sleep on the couch. I could bring down some bedding and—" I don't have to finish.

Margaret nods. "How considerate of you, Oliver. I'd be happy to stay on your couch right by the window. The view here will do me miracles." I hand her the lemonade. Granddad and Earl take their glasses and no one speaks for a while. Earl clearly needs to catch his breath.

"So what exactly are *those*?" Granddad waves his lemonade in the direction of the two blanketed lumps on the floor next to the piano.

"Those, I hope, are the answer to our problem. Trouble is, I know exactly how to work each artifact on its own. I *don't* know how they work *together*. Or *if* they will." Earl hangs his head. "Hedge? How's he doing?"

"He's weak and tired and has marks like your wife," I say rather flatly. But I don't mean disrespect. It's how things are.

"I'm so sorry. I never meant—"

"None of this is your fault. How could you have possibly known?" Granddad moves to look at the wrapped items.

"Well, at any rate, I am sorry. Margaret insisted we come here to see if we could help. The stark truth is we already know Hedge won't be helped by anything medicine has to offer. The one you're standing closest to, Henry, is the camera, which you've already seen. I have supplies for one more photo. The telegraph I acquired a couple of days ago." Earl explains how the telegraph came into his possession. While he and Granddad mutter over the objects, Margaret motions for me to come near.

I help her lie down on the couch and cover her with a light quilt. She smiles, and I smile back. I'm getting used to her face and her deformity and I'm not so shy about making eye contact now. She must have been a beautiful lady at one time.

I sit on the floor near her head so if she speaks, I can hear her requests. She lays a hand on my good shoulder, then moves to tug gently on the strap of the sling. "Tell me what happened, my boy."

I'm not sure if I should burden her, but, much to my aggravation, I tear up. "Please, Oliver. You can tell me anything. See that dear man standing over there? He's tried to protect me from all things evil or slightly irritating for fifty years." She leans a little closer and whispers, "But he doesn't know how strong I am." I look at her, and she attempts a coy wink. This is something she and I have in common—everyone sheltering us.

The weak ones.

"Okay." I sit on the coffee table. I tell her of the attack, and how bad Hedge has become. Bit by bit the story tumbles out, and bit by bit through tears, I feel better. The whole time the old lady holds my good hand in her wrinkled ones. Once she reached up to wipe one of my rogue tears.

"If I were able, dear Oliver, I'd take your granddad's shotgun and put one right between Billy's two front teeth." I laugh out loud. The sight of this frail lady wielding a shotgun, and the surprised look on Billy's face, is almost comical.

We both giggle, which gets the men's attention.

"That, Mr. Andrews," Earl grins and points to us, "looks like a couple of troublemakers if I ever did see."

"That, Earl, is unfortunately accurate," Granddad speaks up for everyone to hear. "Earl and Margaret are welcome guests, for as long as they'd like. He and I are going into town for supplies and ice cream. If you two will behave yourselves while we're gone…"

My heart soars. I'd love to spend more time with Margaret. Even if she dozes off half the time. I sit a little straighter, proud to look over her and fuss after her needs. "I'll take good care of her, Earl, I promise."

"I wouldn't feel a bit comfortable leaving her with anyone else, Oliver."

"No field. Don't touch." Granddad points out to the field and to the floor where he and Earl had wrapped the objects back inside the blankets. "You," he points sternly to me, "are to do *nothing* but care for Margaret while we're gone. No phone. No visitors. Keep the door locked. And Oliver?"

"Yessir."

Granddad whispers, "You know how to use that?" He points toward the front door. Where the shotgun leans in the corner.

I gulp and stare at it. *No, I don't. Never ever touched the thing.* Then I stare at him. I've gone mute. He takes the gun, pumps it, then maneuvers so we're both facing the kitchen.

"It'll knock you on your butt, but you don't have to have good aim to hit something with the spray. Hold it in tight. Here." He pushes the shotgun into my right shoulder. "Pull the trigger with this finger." He tugs at my left index. I wince, more out of fear than pain, as he lifts my left hand, still in the sling next to the loaded gun. "And that lesson'll have to do for now. We'll learn properly once you're healed."

Granddad puts the gun back in the corner. "Oliver?" He says my name rather loudly to jerk me from my trance of disbelief. "Do you understand?"

"Yeah," I say. I take a couple steps toward Margaret and think about whether I could shoot that gun at anything. Or anyone. Then I look at the old lady who's dozed off on the sofa and then to Earl. And I decide right here in the living room, that I could if I had to. "Point and shoot."

Granddad grins. "That about covers it. Well alright then. Earl, you ready?"

Earl kisses his wife's forehead and the men leave.

I look at Margaret, barely a skeleton under the quilt, and I feel more protective over her than I've ever felt over anything.

Granddad and Earl trust me to manage things, sore arm and all. Even if only for an hour. Margaret moans, and I adjust her quilt. I sit in the chair with a view of the lane and the tree line. And here I'll stay until the men return.

I gaze at the shotgun leaning at the ready in the corner. Nothing is going to happen to Margaret on my watch.

I'll make sure of it.

CHAPTER 30

HE COULDN'T BELIEVE his luck. The GPS Knox had planted on Earl's car was pinging from the old farmhouse's yard.

Knox stashed his own vehicle down the road a little closer to the farm and headed for his spot in the tree line. The spot where he'd almost been caught, so he'd camouflaged himself a bit better. Each time he made his way into the brush, the gnats and biting flies were ten times worse than before. Why would anyone live here?

He'd been watching for a while. The two old geezers had left in Earl's car. That tracker, planted back in Chicago, was still live, so he didn't mind. Oliver was probably alone in the house, but he needed to establish a pattern of some sort, so he wouldn't get caught snooping.

He could take Oliver, especially now that he's injured, but he didn't want to *take* him in the violent sense of the word. He wanted to *use* him. He'd spent time and extra money to upgrade his computer for this boonie country yesterday after the disastrous meeting with Billy. He'd needed the time to think and the drive over to the next "city" helped him clear his mind. That town's only electronics store didn't have much, and the feeds from the farmhouse's living room and kitchen remained fuzzy at best. The audio was only slightly better.

The feed on the camera in the wide-open clearing, however,

streamed on, but no one had been there since the kid broke his shovel. Knox would have lived under that light. The clarity and rush it gave him was indescribable. The lamp's magic blended seamlessly with his own.

It was euphoric.

Nestled behind the fallen tree, and now covered in mud, he focused the binoculars on the front window overlooking the porch. The curtains were pulled back, allowing a much better line of sight into that room. He made out Oliver, the pale blue sling giving away his identity. If only Billy had done his job, this would be easier, but Billy failed miserably. Once in a while, Oliver would appear at the window, gazing toward the driveway. Sometimes, he'd peek out the front door. Over and over for the last hour Oliver checked the drive.

He must be OCD, or something. Or he was waiting for Billy, scared out of his mind.

Knox shuffled to relieve a cramp in his leg and knocked a loose branch from a nearby pile of deadwood. He wasn't worried about the noise—he was too far from the house. But the motion…

His heart skipped, and he trained the binoculars on the house. He saw Oliver's slinged form dash across the window.

The porch door opened and Oliver stood, shotgun aimed straight at Knox's head.

He ducked behind the log. If that gun had any kind of scope on it, Knox would be made. Or shot.

Knox held his breath, waiting for gunfire. Two loud bangs almost made him stand with his hands raised in surrender, but he held his position.

He rolled over and lifted his head slowly above the tree trunk. The bangs had come from the screen door slamming, and Oliver was back inside. He rolled back into the mud and exhaled deeply. That was the third time that kid had almost made him.

Knox realized he wasn't going to get close to the house today. He packed his gear up and was heading back to his car, wiping sweat and swatting bugs, when a seed of an idea started to grow and twist and swirl like the vines on the post.

He needed to rid the surrounding farmland of its current owners. Oliver needed his grandfather. If Knox took the land *and* the grandfather, Oliver would need Knox.

Knox imagined Oliver as his loyal protégé. The magic they could harness! What they could accomplish…

It would take time. And conditioning.

And for this plan, Knox needed *Billy* one more time.

CHAPTER 31

I KEEP such close watch on the front of the property that I begin to see things.

A blue Volkswagen Bug.

Billy on foot.

Once, Eddie and Frank strolled out of the corn into the yard dressed in their overalls and ballcaps. Now *that* was something. I must still have some pain meds in my system.

Then movement in the tree line. I *know* I saw that.

I take the gun to the front porch in case something—or someone—did make its way out of the trees. The gun has no scope and if it did, I'm still so sore from beating the lamppost with the shovel that I couldn't lift the shotgun long enough to sight anything through it—not to mention this dumb sling. After waiting for a few moments, I return it to the corner in case Granddad comes home to see me lugging it.

I check on Margaret. Still sleeping, though not at all peacefully.

Earl and Granddad arrive toting groceries and goodies. Evidently Margaret has a sweet tooth when she feels up to eating. I help unpack cinnamon rolls, ice cream and, her favorite, Oreos.

"How'd it go?" Granddad asks.

"Fine." I glance quickly to Margaret in case I let on that I'd seen anything—which now I don't *think* I did. I don't mention the tree line. I don't think there's anything to worry about…

Everyone settles in the living room when Granddad asks if I want to visit Hedge today. "Sure."

"You look tired, though. Are you up to it?"

"Yeah, I've not been taking those pills, so I've been in pain, but it's okay."

Granddad sighs at me. "If we run into Nurse Ratchet, she'll be upset with the both of us."

I grin. "What she doesn't know won't hurt her," I say sheepishly.

"You've been listening to me too long." Granddad makes sure Earl and Margaret have all they need and takes me to the hospital.

Margaret has lifted my spirits. She'd lived a long, difficult life, but ther spunk and kindness today did me wonders. This gives me hope for Hedge.

As we exit the elevator near the waiting area for ICU, I can tell something is wrong. Hedge's parents won't look at me at all, and they glare at Granddad as he goes near them.

"I don't know what kind of stuff you're mixed up in down on your farm, but whatever Hedge got into, it's killing him." Mrs. Conrad lunges at Granddad, and Mr. Conrad catches her by the shoulders.

"Mr. Andrews, Hedge is in a coma," Hedge's dad says as he holds his ex-wife.

I slump against the wall.

"Can I see him?" I'm trying to dam back the tears.

Hedge's mom gathers herself and shrugs. "Don't touch anything, though. They're trying to find a doctor with an opening for him in Chicago. His vitals are stable, but he's—" She can't continue. Sobs overtake her words.

I edge away from them and go to Hedge's room. He has a tube down his throat and several bags of fluid and medication hang above him and off to the side. I didn't know you could have so many cords and wires attached to you and still be alive.

I sit in the chair next to him. "I'm so sorry. I know you said it wasn't my fault, but it is." I wipe tears and snot with the back of my hand, then realize I should wash my hands to avoid giving Hedge any germs.

I walk around the end of Hedge's bed to the sink at the edge of the room, take off my sling, and let the hot water and suds wash over my hands. I turn and study Hedge for a moment. I walk up to the bed and bend down to Hedge's ear.

"I'm gonna *fix* this. You'll see." When I pull away, I notice another red and purple mark similar to Margaret's arm on the edge of Hedge's face along with bruises around his neck and over his throat. I step back, startled, and accidentally drop my sling.

I kneel to retrieve it, and something under the bed catches my eye. I reach back in the dark corner and feel around with my good hand, bracing against the hospital bed with my left and wince from pain.

My fingers finally grasp the round, flat object.

A Volkswagen key chain emblem.

I forget about my shoulder. I forget about my pain. My blood races, sending throbbing pulses through my eardrums.

Billy was here.

CHAPTER 32

WE RIDE to the house in total silence. I think Granddad is upset about Hedge, but there seems to be something else. I dare not tell what I'd found in Hedge's room. I'd tucked the keychain deep into my pocket. I can feel it burning against my leg.

Billy deserves to be punished, but I can't lose Granddad to prison. Granddad *would* kill Billy this time.

Earl and Margaret had gotten along fine while we were gone. Granddad leaves me in charge of serving lunch and goes on to the fields. He has twice as much to do now that Eddie is gone. I'm sure Eddie's family appreciates the help. Especially now.

I plan to do the same for Hedge's mom, if she'll let me.

My arm hurts, but not as bad as the day before. I manage to assemble cold-cut sandwiches to serve to the couple. I tell them about Hedge's condition and how things seem to be out of control. I don't tell them about Billy, though. That's my secret. I wonder if Billy had done something to make Hedge worse. There were bruises on Hedge's neck, but Margaret has similar bruises all over, too.

"Do you have any chickens?" Margaret asks, pulling me back to the living room from the world of what-ifs.

"Yes, but we don't butcher them, they're egg-layers. If you want chicken—"

She grins. "That's not why I'm asking." She wipes her mouth and sits straighter. "I've felt so much better with you, here on this beautiful land."

"What are you getting on about, dear?" Earl prods.

"I'd like some time alone, I think."

"What's that got to do with chickens?" I worry she's delirious.

"Well, if you take that camera and a chicken or two out to the lamppost, you could experiment. I'll stay right here and stall your grandfather, Oliver, should he return before you're back." She says this so matter-of-factly that Earl and I simply stare at her.

"Sweetheart, we're not trying to kill chickens. We're trying to make you better." Earl fusses with her plate and the quilt. She pushes him away and goes into a full sitting position.

"I realize I've not been out and about much in the last few years, but I do accomplish quite a bit of thinking. I think that one artifact plus a lamppost equals trouble—for me and for Hedge. But what if you try it again, only with a chicken and a different object. You used the camera again, the camera caused problems both times—on our wedding day and on the day the boys were in the field. What if you used the telegraph this time? Could it reverse the effects? So, put a chicken under the lamp, take the lens off the camera and see what happens. Then try to reverse what happens with the telegraph."

"You should lie back down, Margaret." Earl seems bewildered.

"It might work," I say.

"Well of course it'll work. Or it won't. But we can't sit here, waiting. We know *that* won't work."

"Well, there's research and documentation to find and—"

"Earl, sweetheart, enough. Time for action, old man. Take young Oliver here, mind his arm now, and Oliver you take Earl, mind his knees now. And you two crippled up gentlemen grab some chickens and start clicking those switches!" She crosses her arms over her chest and Earl moans, but I'm not sure why. At any rate, that last bit of forceful direction takes all the energy Margaret could muster and she lies back flat on the couch.

"Yes ma'am." I look at Earl, silently praying we have a plan of action.

"You'll be okay?" Earl fusses again with Margaret's quilt and pillow.

"Get out of here, I need my rest."

"Decision made, then. Oliver, let's grab some—"

I'm out the back door before Earl can finish the sentence. We have to hurry before Granddad finds out. I crate two chickens—two ladies that haven't been producing eggs in the first place, so they won't be missed if something should happen to them. The thought of hurting them makes me queasy, but Hedge's life, and Margaret's, depends on something, anything, working.

We load Earl's back seat with the chickens. I carefully lay my backpack on the floor boards. Tucked inside, wrapped in thin pillow-cases, are the camera and telegraph. We pray the brass plates won't interact on our way to the light.

We drive the tractor trail, the bumps send pain through my whole body, but the chickens' disapproving squawks help drown out the throbbing. I hope Granddad isn't in this part of the field. I hope he stays on Eddie's side for as long as possible…

I direct Earl as close to the clearing as I can before we're forced to walk the rest of the way.

"I say, I've never had such an adventure. I don't think I've ever been in a field before, let alone in a cornfield. Lived in the city all my life."

"Watch the leaves, they cut." We must look a sight, leaning on each other. One old. One young. Carrying a myriad of objects and two freaked out chickens through the tall stalks.

Earl manages his cane and part of the chicken cage. The backpack strap digs into my sore shoulder and I hope and pray the artifacts won't set each other off. But, it was either do something productive and be in pain or be in pain and stare at the walls waiting for bad news.

We pause a few times to readjust our load and drink. I'm worried the old guy will drop over from dehydration in the high-noon heat. Or that his knees will give out and we'll be stuck here with two screaming hens. He's likely worried about me, too.

What must Earl have experienced all these years, lugging, tugging, and hoping. Trying, failing. Trying again.

Because you may as well try as to not.

We approach the lamppost with some degree of difficulty. We set the crate at the edge of the field.

Earl has a hard time processing the scene, and he breaks down in tears. I put my good arm around his bony shoulders, not quite under-standing. "Are you hurt?"

"No, Son. Not hurt, remembering. Margaret and I got married in a church and afterward, the photographer set us up on the street, under an ornate pole like this one. In the background there was a beautiful shot of the brick and stonework on the church, so directly under the light was the best angle. That's when it happened. That's when—"

"So there was lamppost and a camera back then, too?"

"Same camera, I think. I've tracked it down after nothing else made sense. Different lamppost, but similar." He reaches out to touch the metal pole and he kicks his cane at the bronze plate. "Whoever did this, whatever mind came up with this contraption to deform people and make them sick…"

I haven't thought about the origin of any of this past what Granddad and Eddie relayed in the meeting. Not how it all started. Not who was behind it. Earl's had way more time, though…"I'm just trying to save Hedge."

"Well, then, let's do it."

We sprinkle grain under the light, and I let one chicken out of the crate, calling to her as I do in the yard. She must be hungry because she stays put, pecking away at the feed. We stand back by the corn row and Earl works on the camera, getting the glass and chemicals ready to go. I'm not sure if developing the photo was necessary, but Earl wants to take the same steps.

"Ready?" I nod and Earl aims the camera and takes the lens off. "One one thousand, two one thous—"

Before he can count to three, sparks fly from the camera and the bronze plate on the light. The lamppost comes to life, flashing bright streaks of green into the sky. The chicken squawks in disagreement, thinks about fleeing, but quickly returns to the crushed corn.

And before you can count to three again, it's over.

Earl hurries to apply the chemicals and expose his last photo board against glass plate. Slowly, the image of the chicken appears, her wings mid-stretch and feet mid-stride. "Well, that's a relief," Earl says. "I was almost sure it'd be a cow in Minnesota."

"Now what? Do we wait for the chicken to go into a coma?" I nearly laugh, but it's not funny. Hopefully I could tell Hedge all about this someday, and we'd have a good laugh then. Like in fifty years.

"Not sure, not sure." Earl hobbles over to the chicken. "Does she look okay to you?"

"Yeah, I can't tell anything. It was a while before Hedge showed symptoms, but we don't have a while."

"We should leave her there and try the telegraph. We'll discover if the telegraph creates the same sparks and whether or not it interacts with the lamppost."

We back up to the corn rows once more and Earl worked the telegraph out of the backpack. It is quite amazing. Like something you'd see in black-and-white photos in a history book or behind glass in a museum. The old fashioned lever-and-key system sits on a glossy stained wooden base. The brass plate, though, *that* the telegraph could do without. "You know how that thing works?" We edge toward the corn out of the way.

"Not as well as the camera, but enough to get by." Earl pushes on the lever a couple of times. Sparks from the telegraph's plate and the plate on the pole blow simultaneously. More green beams burst into the sky from the lamp's top.

Earl topples backward, but doesn't fall. He nearly tosses the telegraph onto the ground to pat down his arm where a couple of the sparks landed. A few had signed his beard hair. The lady under the post squawks with disapproval. Her friend in the crate doesn't care for this last show, either, and she starts flailing, feathers flying all over the place.

"It worked, but did it *work*?"

"NASA will not be calling us to join their research team. Let's head back before your Granddad finds out what we've been up to." Earl starts gathering the items into the backpack and grabs his end of the chicken crate. I try to catch the hen under the pole when I notice something I'd not seen before near the glass globe. It almost blends into the raised décor, but it was the wrong shape. The cogwheel designs were all round with raised teeth in the gears, but this was square and smooth. I put my face close to the object, and poke at it with a stick.

"What are you doing? I wouldn't poke at it," Earl warns.

"There's something here."

Earl joins me at the pole. His cane gives a longer reach than my stick and he was able to tap the black square.

"I thought you said not to poke at it."

"I did." Earl grins as he gives the square one final jab with the end of his cane. It falls to the cobblestone and breaks in two. I pick up the parts.

"A camera." I hand it to Earl.

"Not like any camera I've seen. Some newfangled thing."

"Someone's been watching us, Earl. Someone knows what we've been doing today."

Someone like Billy.

CHAPTER 33

KNOX HAD TOLD Billy exactly where to wait. Billy hated this dumb farm, but watching what was about to happen was worth the mosquito bites and sweat rolling into his eyes.

He'd arrived at the farm on foot, his newly purchased hunting knife weighing heavy in his pocket. He'd dashed into the tree line as Oliver and the old geezer Knox warned him about pulled down the lane in the old guy's car and for some odd reason pulled off into the grass by the field.

Granddad was nowhere in sight, but his pickup sat off to the side of the barn. No tractor. He must be in the fields. Once Oliver and the old man cleared out of view, Billy sprang out of the tree line, ran up the drive and rolled out of sight under the pickup. He'd done a little bit of mechanic work in shop class back in high school before he dropped out. Enough to know about brake lines, anyway.

Common sense told him the steep grade at the end of the lane and the reckless way Granddad drives would cause the pickup to increase its speed, sending the old fart across the road and down the ravine.

Billy smiled.

He finished under the truck, peeked around and headed back to the tree line. He nestled against the log, right where Knox said it would be, and waited. He didn't want to miss the outcome of his handiwork. He watched the lane, the edge of the corn, and the house for some time. He glanced at the porch and something caught his eye.

There, in the window, he thought he saw a woman. From this distance, he couldn't be sure. Stick thin with snow-white hair, then she was gone. Just part of her. Half of her. The upper half. The hair stood up on Billy's neck. He didn't believe in ghosts, not really. But what else could that have been?

Granny.

Granny was *watching* him. She'd not been his real grandmother, and she'd never liked him any more than Granddad did. She saw what he'd done to the pickup and now she's haunting him.

He stumbled to his feet, got one shoe stuck in the mud, and barely kept his balance before he stumbled over the pile of dead wood and sprinted out of the trees. He walked back to town sweaty and bug-bitten. He'd had enough of the country.

Back to safety.

He'd not tell Knox about this. Knox's kind, techno-fools, likely don't believe in magic or spooks. He'd report that he'd sliced the line and left the property. Knox was to meet him behind the school. They'd be flagged as junkies, talking in a car with dark tinted windows at a playground, but Knox insisted that's where he wanted to meet. At least the busses had left for the day and the lot was mostly empty.

Billy arrived at the park and found Knox reclined in the driver's seat, AC blasting, going through some old-looking files. He spotted Billy and motioned for him to get in the car.

"Well?"

"Well, I cut the line and left. No big deal."

"You didn't wait to see what would happen?"

"No." Billy shuddered at the thought of the ghost in the window. "Didn't need to. It'll do the trick."

"Better. You didn't do so well last time."

"I did see Oliver and another old guy heading off with a chicken somewhere."

Knox didn't look surprised and rolled his eyes. "Tell me something I don't already know. Anyone else at the farm?"

Billy hesitated. "No. Granddad was gone on the tractor. No one else."

"I think you're lying." He eyed Billy up and down. Billy couldn't help but squirm under Pale Face's glare. "I think you saw something else. You know, if you want to be paid—"

"No, no one else was there, I swear it."

Knox frowned at him and fished out cash from under his seat.

"It's not all here." Billy flipped through the bills.

"Job's not done until dear old Granddad is dead, Billy. I thought I was clear about that."

"He will be."

"When I have proof, I'll pay you the rest. Get out of here before someone sees us together." Knox reached under his seat again, and Billy was afraid he'd pull a weapon this time.

Billy shrugged and left Knox to his files. He walked the three blocks to where he'd parked the Volkswagen. He needed a different plan with this guy. Billy was so worried about the money that he didn't care why his family—well, his step-family—was so important to Knox. At any rate, the pain he'd put Oliver through was worth it. The look on Oliver's face when he finds darling Granddad in the deep, deep ditch will be worth it, no matter if Knox pays him the rest or not.

But that woman.

That figure in the window.

Billy shook off the thought and headed out of town. Knox was coolly cruel, Billy could tell, and didn't take joy in any of the torment he caused. Billy at least enjoyed it, got something out of it.

But what did *Knox* want? What was he trying to gain?

Maybe it was time to find out.

Time to spy on the spy.

CHAPTER 34

KNOX COULDN'T WAIT for Billy to leave. He stank of rotten nature and had drug mud into his car. For now, this car was Knox's home. The least Billy could do would have been to knock off some of the forest before he got in.

He pulled his files onto his lap and began reading again. The air conditioning in the car was giving out; he'd have to drive around town with the windows down to dry off. He didn't want to do that. Didn't want to risk being seen or bothered. He should go back to the tree line and watch for Mr. Andrews' demise, but he also needed to keep an eye on Mr. Jerry Vleet.

Knox had broken into the courthouse last night, so easy to do in these smaller towns. The locks are old, the security system barely second rate. Any idiot with the internet could figure it out. He'd spent hours in the record room, flashlight in mouth, digging through files until he'd found what he wanted. No one would miss what he took. Those records hadn't been touched for years, probably decades. He'd even reset the alarm system so the dear clerk ladies wouldn't be tempted to call anything in.

Knox was a ghost. He could get in and out of brick-and-mortar buildings as easily as he could enter and leave websites and bank accounts.

No one ever knew.

The files led him to the school parking lot. The best place to watch the line of houses, well, one particular house. Jerry's house. He was the only one of the four original farmers who didn't live on the farmland, but in town. Which was good.

Knox had watched Jerry's house all morning. He knew the guy was in there, but he wasn't sure if his wife was home. And, from experience and the failed attempt to boost signals from the farmhouse cameras, Knox didn't bother breaking into Jerry's to plant surveillance.

Since Knox wasn't the kind of person that could pass as a door-to-door salesman, he had to wait. His face was too frightening, or at the very least startling, for most people. He rubbed the back of his neck, gently rolling his fingers over the raised marking of magic, feeling the stress of sitting too long in one position. He put the car in gear and pulled away. Time for a stretch and some dinner from whatever vending machine he could stroll up to unnoticed.

He'd wait until evening. He'd go back to his car parked at the school and retrieve the red vial then, shadowy ghost that he was, he'd slip into Jerry's back door. He'd unscrew the cap from the vial and the homemade mixture, passed from generation to generation through Knox's family, would be dropped onto the old man's forehead as he slept. Jerry wouldn't know a thing. Even if Mrs. Vleet were sleeping next to him, she'd not realize anything was wrong until morning.

Knox grinned again. He would be a ghost. He could feel the power pulsing through his blood, total control. No one else in this small burg knew Knox existed.

No one else but Billy.

And soon, Oliver.

CHAPTER 35

WE'RE bumping along in Earl's car, the chickens unhappy in the back seat, when we see it:

Granddad careening out of control at the end of the lane, pickup swerving too late and plummeting over the ravine. It happens fast, like an action sequence out of a movie. Only the back tires clutch to the top of the ditch.

I jump from Earl's car before he slams the sedan into park. I run toward the pickup, yelling for him to call 9-1-1 from the phone I'd left in my backpack.

Granddad is not moving. A faint line of blood trickles across the steering wheel. With my good arm, I cling to branches and roots until I reach the driver's side door. I balance my foot against the roots, holding the front tire and wish to death that I have two good arms.

I take off my sling and toss it aside. Pain shoots around my scapula, but I don't allow myself to care. And, perhaps because of the adrenaline, soon I don't feel any pain at all, only panic.

I reach for the handle and carefully open the door.

"Careful, Son! Don't move him. He may have broken something. Ambulance is on the way," Earl calls from the top of the ravine.

Granddad tries to raise his head, but I steady him at the nape of the neck. "Careful, Granddad. Don't move. Earl called 9-1-1. Help is coming."

I utter words of encouragement, but somewhere in the middle of them, I break down and sob them out instead of speaking.

Granddad never speaks. He blinks dazed eyes at the shattered windshield.

An eternity passes before the paramedics arrive. They make three attempts before they manage to jostle the stretcher down the awkwardly steep ditch. Earl keeps calling for me to come up, but I don't want to leave.

"It'll be best. You did a good job, Oliver, but we need room to move around." One of the paramedics urges me away.

I pick up my sling from the leaves and mud and make my way up the steep grade to Earl. "It'll be alright. No worries, no worries." Earl hugs me. He whispers into my ear pulling me back toward the car. "Let's go put the chickens back and check on Margaret. I'll drive you straight to the hospital after." It feels cruel to leave like this, but I know he's right. I slide into the passenger seat of the sedan.

Numb from head to toe.

At the ER reception area, I ask the nurse for Granddad's location. Earl accompanies me in, then heads back to the house to tend to Margaret. And I'm glad.

I want to be alone with Granddad. I also don't want Margaret to be alone. She'd been fine for the little while we were in the field, but leaving her for long stretches wouldn't be good.

A nurse leads me to a curtained area where two more nurses and the paramedic from the ravine work on Granddad. He has a gash on his forehead and purple welts on his cheeks. His arm is in a pale blue sling, and when he tries to speak, he grimaces. He raises his slinged arm slightly and mutters "Twins."

Relief floods over me.

It's a strange sensation. Relief. When the body's been so tense and tight for so long. My muscles relax and I exhale as if I've been holding my breath for days.

I shudder when I think about what could have happened. The ravine runs the length of that road across from our farm and follows along the road in either direction for miles. Several people have gone over, especially when the roads ice over in the winter. And where there aren't enough trees hugging the bank, the ones who go over in those spots, well, they don't make it out.

"What happened?"

"I was coming here to check on Hedge. Got a call…" He trailed off as he began to speak. The nurses scowl at me, but I'm not about to leave Granddad's side. "Anyway, headed down the lane, pushed on the brake and nothing happened. No brakes, went over."

Bad luck and bad news. Every day brought some new worry or catastrophe. "I'm sorry, Granddad."

"Not your fault. Billy's fault probably."

"Billy?"

"Margaret saw someone in the lane. She'd sat up to stretch and thinks she saw something out in the trees. She's got keen eyesight to go with her keen mind. For an old gal." He reaches up to rub his forehead and winces again.

"How do you know it was Billy?"

"Who else could it be? Looking and lurking around? Ouch!" A nurse jabs a needle into his arm.

"Antibiotics. And you need rest. We should file a police report, Mr. Andrews, if you believe someone caused this accident."

"No police. I'll take care of my own business. And I'll rest at home—"

The nurse cuts him off. "No, you won't. We're keeping you for observation. You've got a nasty head wound and probable concussion. You'll rest here."

He glares at the nurse and throws his good arm in the air. "I'll stay here, but I'll not rest here. All the poking and checking—"

"I'll stay here with you, Granddad. And I can check on Hedge, too."

"No, we have guests. Hedge is worse, Oliver, that's why I was on my way here." Granddad moans as he repositions himself in the bed. "His mom called. A doctor from Chicago can check him, but Hedge is too weak to be moved. They're battling insurance and whether the doctor should come here or Hedge should go there."

Oliver slumps down into the chair next to the bed. "He can't leave, Granddad. Earl and I, well, we're working on an idea."

"Have you been in the field again?" Granddad almost comes out of the bed. He rips off the blood pressure cuff and an alarm goes off, bringing the nurses back to the room in a hurry.

"Lie still, sir. Young man, you'll have to leave if you're aggravating him," said the nurse as she looks over the rim of her glasses at me.

"He's not, and I'd like to have a conversation with my grandson, if you don't mind."

"Just a while longer. But keep still." The nurse reapplies the cuff and leaves the room with a huff.

"Oliver?"

"We had an idea, Granddad. One that might work. One that could help Hedge and Margaret. If we fix this, we can work on getting Dad and Mom back and then call the police on Billy and then—"

Granddad holds up his good arm again and leans back in the bed. "Okay, slow down. No police. We'll handle our own matters with Billy. The police around here, well, they work for us anyway." He sees the confusion race over my face and changes the subject. "I guess things can't get much worse for Hedge—or Margaret for that matter. Tell me your idea."

I relay the events from the east field up until Earl and I watched him go over the ravine.

"So you don't know what happened with the chicken?"

I shake my head. "Earl was going to keep an eye on things until I could get back and we could talk with you." I sit on the edge of the seat, unsure what reaction the story will bring from the banged-up old man.

Granddad is quiet a minute. "Oliver, I'm gonna need my cell

phone. It's probably still in the truck, so be careful. You bring it to me first thing in the morning, okay?" I nod, but I imagine the truck is still in the ditch and that would mean another trip down the ravine, hugging the vehicle with one good arm. "Now, go up and see Hedge and then run home and make sure everything there is okay before it gets too dark outside. I don't want you walking around alone at night with Billy up to who-knows-what. Understand?"

"Okay, then what?"

"In the morning, when our heads are clear and we've had some rest, we'll think of something." He rubs his head, and winces. "Or, the way things are going, the next step might fall into our laps." He gives my hand a squeeze.

"I'm glad you're alive. I don't want anything to happen to you." I lay my head on Granddad's chest in a gentle half-hug.

"I don't want anything to happen to you either, Oliver." Granddad tears up. I don't like this side of him. Truth is, since that Friday in the barn when I caught him tearing up, Granddad's been going soft off and on all week. I love the hard-nosed farmer the most—his emotion scares me. "Now get. Before it gets dark."

I get my feet under me and aim my best "good boy" smile to the angry nurse, Nurse Angela W., at the reception area. I try to avoid drawing attention to myself as I exit the elevator upstairs, especially attention from Hedge's mother. I don't want a confrontation full of accusations for this again, even if it is my fault.

"Oliver?"

Unfortunately, hoping is futile. Mrs. Conrad was sitting around the corner. "I was going to peek in. Granddad is here 'cause of an accident or I wouldn't bother you—"

"That's okay." She puts down her magazine on the table and meets me in the hallway. "He's doing no better. He's losing a lot of weight, even though they're feeding him through the IV. The nurses don't want us in there for long stretches at a time, fearful of infections, I guess." She tears up.

"I won't go in, then. I don't want to cause…" I stop myself. There is nothing more I can say to her that will make her feel better.

"His dad and I are getting back together though." She brightens. "We've had a lot of time to discuss our issues while we sit here, waiting. We're moving back to Chicago."

Those last words punch me hard. If Hedge dies, I lose my friend. If Hedge lives, I lose my friend.

I try to smile, "That's great news. I'm sure Hedge will be so happy."

"Thanks. Go on in and see him, but keep it short." She pats me on the shoulder and I wince. The adrenaline has washed out of my system, and the pain signals fire again.

Hedge's face is thinner than it was just a few days ago. He's lifeless. I squeeze his hand and whisper close to his face, "We're gonna fix this. Me and Earl. We're gonna figure it out, I promise." Hopefully before Billy can do any more damage. I keep my promise to keep the visit short. I would've stayed till dawn, but Hedge probably can't hear me anyway.

As I step out into the steamy evening, I have about an hour before the sun sets. The air is heavy with humidity and weighs on my mood. I glance around the lot for Billy's Volkswagen, which isn't in sight, but *not* seeing it doesn't bring comfort. I think about circling back to the ER to sit with Granddad one more time, but I know I have to go home. I try to shake off the emotions, the pain in my shoulder, and the growing sting of acid in my stomach.

I head toward the school, ready to cut through the back lot and shave some time off the hike to the farmhouse. A black car with dark, tinted windows sits in the lot. I've not seen that car at school before, at least not that I can remember.

No one should be in the school lot at this hour unless there was an evening event. And there wasn't one. A figure gets out of the car, and I quicken my pace, trying to decide whether or not to change directions. The man is dressed in all black. His pale skin glows in the dimming summer evening.

I try not to gawk at him, and then remember the dark figure from the day of the funeral. The one who'd sat in Billy's car.

I direct my footsteps toward the front of the school, hoping I'd not been spotted. This is surely Billy's buddy.

Sure now that I need to take the long way home, I start to jog. I have less than an hour to traverse the dark county road to the farm.

Less than an hour to go before I would be safe in the house with Earl and Margaret.

For the first time I can remember, I'm more scared of what people may be lurking in the dusk than what hungry coyotes may be lurking in the cornfields. All wanting a pound of my flesh.

I take a break halfway to the farm to throw up in a ditch. As I'm wiping my mouth off on my shirt hem, I hear tires behind me.

I sprint the rest of the way home.

CHAPTER 36

EARL SAT with his wife on the sofa when Oliver burst through the front door. "How's your Granddad?" Earl began to ask, then he processed the distress on Oliver's face. "Oh, my. What happened?"

Oliver was rummaging in the fridge; he was winded and sweaty. Once the boy caught his breath, he slumped into the living room chair and told Earl everything that happened at the hospital.

"My, my. Things keep getting more complicated. You sure you didn't recognize the man at the school?"

Oliver shook his head.

"Do you mind if I light my pipe? Thanks. It helps me think." He reached into his right vest pocket for the tobacco pouch and stuffed a pinch into his favorite pipe. He kept a tiny wooden box of matches in his left vest pocket, struck one and held the flame and sucked on the pipe until the spark took.

Margaret rolled her eyes. "You'd be better off quitting that habit, dear."

"Well, honey, it's gotten me this far." He winked at Oliver. "Now then, let me tell you about that chicken. Nothing. Nothing happened. Good, bad, or otherwise. The little lady is fine so far as I can tell. You may want to check on her, though. You no doubt know more than I about such matters with chickens."

"I trust you. I'm not trying to be rude. I'll check on the hen in the morning before I go back to the hospital. Goodnight Margaret. I hope you sleep well." Oliver shook Earl's hand and tapped Margaret's lightly.

"Goodnight, sweet boy." Margaret waved at Oliver as he went up the stairs. She turned to her husband, "We've gotten them into some kind of mess, haven't we?"

Earl took a long drag on his pipe, slowly letting the smoke free of his mouth until it swirled above his head in white ribbons. "I'm afraid so. We can do another test with the chickens and then see—"

"No. It's time, Earl. To do something different. I don't want to sacrifice any more chickens—or lives—on my behalf."

"What are you saying?" Earl's brow furrowed.

"I'm tired, hon." She took his hand in hers. He extinguished the pipe and held her with both hands, waiting for her to go on. "You have time to have a life. I'm done. I want… *peace*."

"Oh, no. No, no." He reached for her face and brushed away a tear from her wrinkled cheek. "What are you saying?" Earl knew already, but he didn't want to face it.

"You've done all you can. And these last days have been so wonderful, I've never felt so alive—"

"Then don't give up, let's—"

She took both his hands and her dulling blue eyes met his. "I love you Earl Carl Edwards. You are my one true love; my soulmate given to me by God himself. You have taken amazing care of me, never wavering. And now, do something for yourself, for my sake. I'm asking you, please let me go."

Earl buried his face in his wife's frail lap. He could feel her run her hands through his white hair and across his shoulders. He couldn't lose her. Not here. Not this way. Not after they were so close.

"Take me to the light. Let *me* be the next guinea pig. No more chickens, no more boys. If I get better, even a little bit better, bring

Hedge to the post. If I don't, please let me go in peace." She nudged him up to make sure he understood.

His kind eyes were bloodshot, spilling tears on her white night-gown. He hung his head and nodded in agreement. "I love you. You are my wonderful gift. I will love you forever."

Earl spent the rest of the night on the couch next to his beloved wife. His best friend. His soulmate.

For tomorrow he would help fulfill her selfless wish. She was sacrificing herself to save a young boy's life.

CHAPTER 37

I'M awake before the sun is. I dress quickly and bound down the stairs to see Earl and Margaret still on the couch. "You alright?" Earl looks despondent, and Margaret weaker than I've seen her since she'd been to the farm. She was attempting to eat breakfast, but struggling to bring the food to her lips.

"Yes, Oliver. And we have a new plan. Come with me." Earl squeezes Margaret's hand, and crosses into the kitchen where he tells me about taking Margaret to the lamppost.

"But Earl, she's too weak. She won't—" I gasp back a sob. Earl hugs me and we both melt down.

"This is what she wants. She wants to help your friend. She wants to be at peace. Will you help me?"

"Of course. I've got to fetch Granddad's phone from the truck and take it to him—"

"Oh, my dear boy. I'm afraid we'll need to go right away. Before this old geezer changes his mind and hauls his wife back to Chicago." Earl smiles through tears.

"Okay. Right away." I'm dumbfounded. I feel as if I'm about to take Margaret to the slaughtering block. Nothing happened to the chicken, but the old woman may not survive the ride through the field.

I glance into the living room. Margaret catches me and crosses her arms over her chest in defiance and winks. *Okay then.*

Over the next half hour, as the sun rises, we wrestle her and the telegraph into Earl's car, but not without great difficulty. With Earl's bad knees and my weak shoulder, we almost lose our grip on her as we struggle on the porch steps.

I sit in the back with Margaret on the way to the light, holding her around her thin shoulders, trying to soften the bumps and dips in the tractor lane. She leans near my ear. "No worries, Oliver. This is the best adventure I've been on in a lifetime!" She grins her half-faced grin and I can't help but laugh. She reaches up and brushes my freckles, no doubt bright orange.

When the car goes as far as it can on the grassy swath, Earl parks and looks back. Now for the walk through the corn—with a wheelchair.

Try as we might to shield her from the razor-sharp stalks, Margaret ends up with a couple of scratches on her face. Her paper-think skin is no match for even the slightest brush of leaves.

The chair's wheels become stuck in the mud multiple times and we tug and push through. Once we almost bounced Margaret right out of the seat.

What a sight we must be. Earl in a suit. Me in a sling. Margaret in a nightgown and housecoat.

We stop many times between the car and the post. We do our best to keep her drinking and comfortable. The sun is barely up, but we didn't need to take her quilt from the house. The heat is blanket enough.

She sees the lamppost and gasps.

"Earl, it's just like the one—"

"Yes, dear, I know."

She turns to me, the biggest smile spreads on her face. "We had our wedding portraits done under a light like this one."

"Don't look so happy about it, dear. That wasn't one of the best days ever."

"Yes, it was. And don't you ever say otherwise. Onward!" She points her arm out in front of her as if directing the Cavalry.

We wheel her under the light. Earl and I wince more than she does as the wheelchair bumps across the unyielding brick and pebble. She reaches out and runs her fingers over the scrollwork.

"Wait." "No!" Earl and I speak at the same time.

She shoots us an eye roll and ignores our warning. "What's it going to hurt *now,* boys?"

We take our scolding and retreat to the corn's edge with the telegraph. "I don't think I can do this, will you?" Earl thrusts the telegraph into my hands. I push it back. Earl repeats the motion, holding firm with a stern tilt of his head until I take the device.

Earl mimics how to work the lever and key and shows me where the switch is.

"Ready? Here goes." I press the lever and flip the switch. The lamppost doesn't fail. It whizzes and lights, sparks fly from both bronze plates and a few bounce off the wheelchair's metal footrest. When the green glow and sparks subside, we rush back to the old woman.

She is smiling, well half-smiling. "Oh, Earl. That was amazing! Can we do it again, do you think?"

"Not a chance. Oliver needs to be back at the hospital." She doesn't argue with this reasoning. We start the trek back to the car when I notice the corn rustling about twenty rows down. I wait and watch for the rustle to ripple through the rest of the rows, like it does when the breeze is blowing. But there is no ripple effect. The air isn't moving. No breeze.

Earl breaks my gaze. "A little help here, son?" I turn my attention back to holding the stalks' leaves away from Margaret's face and arms.

All the way home, Margaret chats. Constantly. About their first date. About their wedding plans and all the guests at the wedding.

"Slow down, there girl. You're gonna run out of breath." Earl looks hopefully at his wife in the rearview mirror. "Maybe this worked, Oliver. I've not seen her so bright."

I study Margaret's asymmetrical face and the red raised mark on her hand as she rambles on about her earlier years. Nothing's changed outwardly. At least it doesn't appear that our "experiment" did her any harm.

But the closer we get to the farmhouse, the corn scratches *did* change. The same cuts that had been bleeding from her cheeks moments ago now appear several days old.

By the time we reach the yard, the scratches have healed.

I tingle from my head to my feet. My stomach flutters. My left arm doesn't hurt nearly as it did before all this jostling. My heart races and thuds and doesn't quite know what to do with itself.

As Earl pulls the car onto the driveway, I've made a decision.

I'm breaking Hedge out of the hospital.

CHAPTER 38

THEY PUSHED the ghost into the corn. The ghost he'd seen in the window of the farmhouse.

Well, at least he wasn't crazy. Billy *had* seen something. What were they doing? Everything had sparked and crackled under the odd pole. He went to inspect the area. He didn't know how to turn the light on. He didn't have the other piece Oliver used. Some remote control, or something.

Billy figured Oliver was into something illegal. Where else would he have gotten the money to pay for his little travels in Chicago that day? He'd probably found a way to "heal" people and rip them off. And if Oliver knew how this stuff worked, Knox probably did, too, because Knox dripped of money.

They must've been in on the endeavor together, but Knox is greedy and wants it all to himself. That's why he hired Billy to move Oliver out of the way.

Well, now *Billy* knew. What an opportunity! He circled the pole, poking at it here and there and bent to touch some engraving at the bottom. The plate burned his fingers and he took a few steps back.

Billy thought himself rather creative. He would make good with Granddad, take over the farm and plow it all down to a parking lot.

He'd market it and make a fortune by the end of the year. First he had to get rid of Knox. For some reason, that man didn't have enough sense to know what he was dealing with.

He knew where Knox had parked. He started back to the tractor track through the corn, trying to take the same path the old geezers and Oliver had taken in case they dropped something. He didn't find anything.

He walked the track back to the road where he'd parked his Volkswagen and drove to the school lot. Knox was in his car, playing with his high-tech toys, as usual. Toys probably bought with the funds from the clandestine secret pole in the middle of nowhere.

Billy knocked on the window. Knox slowly rolled it down. "What do you need? Why are you here?" He barely looked at Billy, which infuriated him. No respect.

"I know your secret. And I want in."

"What secret?" Billy had Knox's attention now.

"The sparking light in the cornfield. The light that heals old women in wheelchairs and makes you tons of money. The one that Oliver is helping you run. *That* secret."

Knox exited the car and calmly stretched. "You mean, Oliver was busy again today? With an old woman? And with a bad arm?"

"Didn't look too sore. Must've used the pole to heal himself."

Knox rolled his eyes subtly, but Billy caught the slight. He balled his hands in a fist, ready to knock Pale Face to the ground. "Well, I guess he did. And I suppose you'll want cash?"

Billy was surprised. He'd readied himself for a fight. "Uh, sure."

"Well, you must understand how everything works before I let you in. It's complicated." He pointed to the car full of high-tech gear. "And, like you said, a secret. So, first thing is you must swear to not tell anyone."

"Agreed." Billy shivered. He was entering into a contract that would make him a ton of money.

"Second thing. Your first lesson must be at the lamppost. I'll meet you there with your cash." Knox reached through the open car window and rummaged for a second. He handed Billy a phone.

"I'll call you. Let you know what time I can meet you there. You, know. For the first lesson."

Billy's eyes widened. "No problem."

"I've got work to do." Knox got back into the car without looking at Billy. He rolled up his window and started the engine but didn't go anywhere. Knox sat there, staring at the laptop with the AC running.

Billy hated Knox. But, he wouldn't need him long. After his training, Billy was sure he could run things on his own.

He turned to his rusting Volkswagen and smiled despite the hunger rumbling in his stomach. Hunger for more than just a greasy meal down at Darla's Diner. Hunger for revenge. Hunger for power.

Hunger for money.

He circled with his thumb across the driver's side window, creating a smiley face in the accumulated road dust.

Soon, Billy could afford tinted windows.

CHAPTER 39

EARL AND OLIVER helped Margaret back into the farmhouse. Earl had taken off his vest and jacket and left them in the sedan. The humid swelter and his second adventure to the lamppost finally forced him to untuck his shirt tail and roll up his sleeves.

He offered Margaret the quilt once she was settled on the sofa. She waved it off, smiling. "I'm not cold, dear."

Earl certainly wasn't cold, either. So many months and years of dealing with chills and shakes—from old age and anxiety, and now, Earl trembled on the inside from the trek. He wiped sweat from his forehead with his sleeve. He'd reached for his handkerchief, but it was stuffed into the pocket of his jacket. He also went for his pipe and tobacco, but those old friends were also in the car. Margaret was right. He should work on cutting back…

Oliver had poured them all some lemonade and ran upstairs to shower before Earl was to drive him to the ravine—much against Earl's good judgment—to retrieve Henry's phone, and then on to the hospital.

He sat by his wife. Neither spoke for a long time. Neither looked at one another, either. They sat and sipped and caught their breath.

And processed.

Only a week ago, their routine was tending to Margaret's suffering and Earl's searching. Now, everything had changed.

Here. In the middle of nowhere. In this glorious isolation. Something was different…

They both startled a bit as Oliver thumped around above their heads. Earl looked at Margaret. She smiled.

His heart skipped a beat. Not because her smile had never done that to him before—it had always sent his heart out of rhythm. Especially when her eyes lit up with the sideways upturn of her lips.

This time though, her smile was different.

This time, *both* sides of her mouth turned up.

She examined him. She reached for the end of his shirt tail and jiggled the rolled-up cuff with her hand. The twisted scar wasn't so twisted any longer. It was beginning to fade. He gawked at her wide-eyed, lemonade glass toppling to the hardwood floor with a crack.

Oliver bounded down the stairs shortly after the commotion. "Is everything—"

Oliver stopped mid-sentence, dropped his backpack to the floor and stood rubbing his shoulder and shaking his head.

"Well, aren't you boys just gobsmacked." Margaret giggled, rose from the couch, gathered the broken shards and took them to the kitchen.

Earl stood next to Oliver, both of them watching Margaret as if she was a waxwork mannequin suddenly come to life.

She turned back to the living room, arms crossed over her chest.

"Why are you still standing there? Go get Hedge!"

CHAPTER 40

KNOX WAITED at the ravine near the top of the steep bank, nestled among the brush. This afforded him the best line of sight to the wrecked pickup, but it was out of sight of the road. He'd thought about shimmying down the hill and rummaging the pickup for the phone for himself, but then he'd thought better of it.

Patience had paid off greatly for Knox so far. So he'd let patience serve him once again.

While he waited, he tossed the second vial he'd concocted in as many days from one hand to the next. Then he spun it between his long, pale fingers.

Tick, tick, ticking the time away.

Looking forward to the day when he'd stop stalking and waiting and start doing. Doing the bidding of the magic that flowed through his veins.

He held the blue vial up to the sunlight streaming through the tree canopy. Just enough. Not too much. Not too little. It'd only take a drop.

Knox thought about Jerry's red vial, now lying empty on the back floorboard of his car. He'd refill it for Oliver's grandfather if need be, but he doubted it would come to that.

Knox simply needed Oliver.

He reached for his back pocket—force of habit—for his cigarettes and lighter, then remembered he was out. All the better. The aroma of cigarettes would clue anyone around here into his presence. He tucked the blue vial into his front pocket and pulled out the lighter.

Flick. Flame. Flick.

Tick, tick, ticking the time away.

He'd been here since Billy relayed the messages about the old woman at the pole. Oliver and Earl had destroyed his camera, and the ones in the house weren't functioning beyond flashing black-and-white static flecks and the occasional blurred image. He'd wasted his time upgrading his equipment—at least for visual aids.

He was sick to death of the country and its poor connectivity to things that mattered. If his ancestors had seen fit to bestow upon him the great burden of mystery, you'd think they'd also have the foresight to nudge someone along to put up a few extra cell towers in parts like these.

One bit of news *did* come through on the audio after Billy left him in the school lot. When the garbled voices floated through his laptop's speakers, he imagined the lamppost was communing with him. Lining things up just so. So Knox could be in the right place at the right time.

Something about a phone in a ravine. Evidently, Overalls was sending Oliver down to the truck to retrieve a cell phone. He'd also picked up a fairly strong female voice, but he couldn't place the character. Maybe the mother was back. Maybe Eddie's widow…

The audio cut out again shortly after. The post in the field with its brass plate and streaming sparks of wonder had given Knox exactly what he'd needed for the next step.

He retrieved the vial from his pocket and wiggled it through the fingers on his right hand. With his left, he flicked the lighter again.

Flick. Flame. Twist. Wait.

Repeat.

Staking out the wrecked pickup afforded him the best opportunity to introduce himself to Oliver. With Hedge in the hospital and the other players in this game being over seventy years old and decrepit, Oliver would surely have to scale the ravine on his own to retrieve the phone.

And Knox would lend him a hand.

CHAPTER 41

MARGARET IS RIGHT. I am gobsmacked. More like gobslugged. Earl and I are frozen in time and to the floor, watching her flit and dart around the house, folding up quilts and tidying the remnants of the lemonade and the morning's breakfast.

The morning's breakfast when she was barely able to bring the fork to her crooked mouth. Now she smiles at us, a beautiful, symmetrical smile.

Earl finally speaks. "Margaret, dear. Maybe you should slow down a bit."

She takes an armload of dishes to the kitchen and comes back to the living room. She pulls out the piano bench, sits down and plunks a few of the keys, mismatched comical notes tumble from the instrument. "I've been slowed down for decades. I feel so…alive." She squares up to the piano, places both hands on the keys and plays. A melodious piece that I've never heard before.

Earl stands with his mouth hanging open, rubbing his beard with one hand and the top of his head with the other. "Our wedding song," he mumbles.

She stops playing and turns around to face us. "I meant it about Hedge. You'd better hurry up." She stretches her arms in front of her body and examines them as if they are two strangers hooked to her body. She brings her hands up closer to her face. Hands that are still wrinkled with the passing of time, but no longer marred with bruises and that wicked scar.

I look at Earl. And I could see it in his face. I know he doesn't want to leave her. Not now.

He's gotten his wife back.

I put a hand on his shoulder. "I'll go down and get the phone from the truck and walk to the hospital to see Granddad and Hedge. You, um, stay here with Margaret for a while. I'll call you on the landline when I've figured out what to do about Hedge and whether I can even move him or not."

Earl only nods as he slides down to the piano bench next to his wife. She turns back to the keys and picks up the melody where she'd left off. I stand for a bit, taking in the sight until the stress of it all catches up with me and I think I see sparks coming from under the piano behind the foot pedals.

I see sparks everywhere now. And sometimes dead people walking out of the corn rows.

I grab my backpack, stuff in some water bottles, and toss in a rag to wipe the sweat and grime that's sure to accumulate on me during the hike to the hospital.

I don't look forward to the climb into the ravine nor the trek into town on foot. Not after being so spooked the last time I hoofed it back from town in the dark.

I step onto the front porch and let the screen door slam shut behind me. The sun is high, and though it's blistering hot, there's not a cloud in sight and I've plenty of daylight. No coyotes to worry about.

No one can lurk in shadows when there are no shadows.

CHAPTER 42

I REACH the ravine in short order and drop my backpack at the top of the ditch near the road and leave my sling—now stained with sweat and field dust and who knows what else. It'll just get in the way and I need to hurry. This week's events and today's tasks run races through my brain and propel me forward. Forward to Granddad. To Hedge. To the farm.

To the lamp post.

I scale the sharp incline down toward Granddad's truck. I'm surprised the vehicle hasn't slid further down the hill and on into the creek below. Thick roots and various diameters of saplings suspend the truck on the side of the hill. I grab at some smaller branches and do a clumsy sideways scissor-step down to the driver's side door, which hangs open from the EMTs' rescue. The passenger's side is blocked by thorny shrubs and scraggly saplings.

No doubt the truck is a total loss. Busted front end. The door pried open by the rescue workers.

Busted windshield with Granddad's dried blood color coordinating with the rust on the exterior. I swallow hard. I wonder if the driver's side seat belt had been in working order if Granddad would've been in the hospital at all—maybe an arm injury, but likely not a concussion.

I shake off the intrusion and grab the hand rest in the opened door with my sore arm and carefully lean into the truck. Papers, wrinkled and stained light brown, litter the floorboards. Granddad's coffee thermos is wedged between the dash and the passenger's side of the front glass. A faint crack extends on that side where the metal thermos must've shot from the seat beside him like a bullet as he went over the ditch. Stale coffee, damp forest floor, and a faint hint of gasoline fill my nostrils.

The little black cell phone is nowhere to be seen. Granddad thought he'd been talking on it as he went over, so it wouldn't be in the glove box or middle console. Probably on the floor under the papers.

I balance my right foot on the floorboard's edge and reach as far as I can with my good arm, left arm barely clinging to the door. I move the papers to the side but have to adjust my grip to get a better view. Before I can catch myself, my left hand moves to grip the steering wheel.

The wheel turns. Ever so slightly, but it turns.

The rusted machine creaks under me, grumping about its plight and ultimate fate to wither away to nothing over the next century here in this ravine.

I forget about being careful and lunge toward the opposite floorboard, scouring and searching like mad with my right hand until I feel the cold of the phone tucked up under the seat.

I wriggle backward, trying not to bump the steering wheel, but it's too late. My legs are free of the cab and my feet grip the uneven hillside, but my torso is not quite loose before the truck takes a slow roll toward the creek.

With a death grip on the cell phone, I stumble away from the pickup, but not fast enough to clear my right shoulder from the cab before I'm pinned.

I take a few sideways steps toward the creek, dancing awkwardly with the wrecked truck. The roots and saplings give up their final grip and the truck picks up speed.

With all my might I pull backward. I hear my shirt rip and feel pain in my right shoulder, but I'm free. I stumble up, trip over a root and land on my butt. The phone flies from my hand into the forest debris of leaves and sticks and rutted-up dirt scooped into position by the pick-up's course last night. Right where the truck had been resting only seconds ago.

I sit stunned and bleeding, watching Granddad's prized pickup speed hood-first into the creek below with a loud crash against the creek's stony bank. The gasoline fumes are stronger now.

And I feel heat. Popping and cracking from my right. Where the phone landed.

I pull myself from my trance and try to balance, one foot a good two feet higher than the other on the steep bank side. I step toward the ruts to dig for the phone before the baby flames grow into adulthood, but I lose my footing.

I try again with the same result, sliding several feet toward the truck. I struggle against the roots and saplings that will me to roll into the line of fire.

The flames grow, sending a narrow snake of knee-high orange flames all the way to the creek. Flames lick the underside of the pick-up's bed and send smothering smoke wafting up the hill and into my face.

I turn back to the wreck site, my eyes burn and water and my feet slip. I see a dark form standing in front of the dancing flames.

A pair of outstretched hands offering hope.

One of those hands holding Granddad's phone.

CHAPTER 43

KNOX SAW it happen and moved quickly. Like a ghost in one fluid motion.

He'd tucked the blue vial safely in his pocket as the kid scaled down the hill. He wouldn't need it yet. A few more steps first…

As soon as he saw the truck inch forward from its resting place, he moved.

His ancestors smiled on him. Blessed him with this glorious opportunity.

Knox knew the slow gasoline drip from the wrecked pickup had been their doing. Maybe his father's very own plan. He could see his father smiling.

Then Knox smiled and slithered his way to the passenger side of the accident site. But it wasn't an accident, now was it?

He could see his father's father smiling. Knox flicked the lighter near the debris and picked up the phone as Oliver was busy trying to gather himself after extricating himself from the pickup.

Now his grandfather's father joined in the ancestral reunion. What pride he had in that moment. A sense of belonging.

A sense of purpose.

He was so close.

Knox stood with his back to the flames and offered himself to Oliver.

I can't see who's helping me. I don't care. I need out of the ravine. I need the phone. I need to get to Granddad and Hedge. I reach up with two sore arms and the dark-clad stranger pulls me to my feet.

I rub my irritated eyes and cough, half clinging onto this silhouette, half stumbling on my own up and out of the ravine. Away from the flames. From the memories. From yet another failed attempt at help.

Knox helped Oliver to the road. As Oliver struggled with the climb, Knox thumbed through the phone. Not much battery left and not much hill left, so he'd have to be fast.

Summon his ancestors for one more favor.

Oliver stumbled into him at one point during their ascension, nearly knocking the phone out of Knox's hand. But he held tight. To the kid and the cell.

There was only one number in the phone. Oliver bumped into him again.

What luck. He wouldn't have to bother stealing the thing later, and he could commit this single number to memory easily enough.

When they reached the roadside, while Oliver's back was to him, he studied the number, intent on memorizing it while Oliver fussed with his backpack.

But Knox wouldn't have to memorize it. He wouldn't have to call in another favor from his family.

He already knew the number by heart.

We reach the side of the road at the top of the ravine. I can make out my backpack and my dirty blue sling sitting by the ditch. I'm still coughing. Eyes still on fire.

The stranger pats my back. His hand are like ice. I can feel the cold through my shirt. Maybe it's because I'd been so close to the flames.

I grab my sling and rub my eyes with it, something that hadn't been tainted with smoke and fumes, and I rummage in my backpack for the water bottles.

When I find my voice, I squeak out a shaky "thank you" and I turn to hand one of the bottles to the stranger.

He takes his icy fingers off my back and looks me in the face.

He takes the water.

And smiles.

Then, without a word, the palest man I've ever seen—the same man from the school parking lot last night—hands me Granddad's phone, turns, and walks away.

CHAPTER 44

REMAINING IN A STATE OF CONSTANT "GOBSMACK," as Margaret would put it, is exhausting. Everything about this week, the farm, Granddad. Everything. And now this perfectly pale stranger.

I walk, well, more like slink, my way to town. The afternoon sun cooks the shirt to my back, like it does in the middle of the fields when I ride alongside Granddad on the old tractor. As the sun always does.

That one constant from before I knew about magic lampposts. Before I knew how to point and shoot. Before my friend was dying.

Before the icy touch of the man's hand.

I reach with my right hand to try to soothe the area where he'd patted me. My ripped shirt had stuck to the freshly clotted wound, and the motion pulls the sleeve and I bleed again. I don't think the cut is deep, but arriving at the hospital like this will send Granddad into a ruckus.

And the ruckus will escalate when I have to tell him about the fire because I reek of smoke.

I'd stood at the top of the road for what felt like an eternity before heading toward Fallston "city" limits. My gaze would drift between the shrinking silhouette of the pale-faced man and the dying flames down the ravine. I'd flipped the phone open, ready to call 9-1-1, not for myself, but in the event the fire needed tending to. But I hadn't needed to make that call.

With the recent downpours and the dampness of the ravine, the fire didn't last long. All that was left when I turned toward town were a few patches of wispy smoke.

And the stranger had disappeared around the S-curve well past our gravel drive.

I reach into my jeans pocket and feel for the cell phone that caused this current struggle. I guess I should be grateful for the stranger. Without him, I'd have lost the phone completely.

I hope Granddad really did need it. I flip it open again and go to the contacts. Only one number.

Must be some uber important number.

I arrive at the front of the hospital, ragged, dirty, and quite literally torn. Inside and out.

A young nurse leaves the bench she was resting on and comes running up to me. "Oh, my word. Let me help you in here."

"It's okay, just a scratch. I'm here to see my granddad and my friend."

Her name badge says *Angela Y.* Hedge was right. Too bad she's working on *his* floor.

She wraps an arm around me and leads me to the ER, again with the ER. Where Nurse Evil, Angela W., sees my sling hanging from my bleeding right hand instead of supporting my bad left shoulder.

"I'm sorry," the nice Angela says. "I have to get back to ICU, but the ER staff will take good care of you." She winks at me. "You're Hedge's friend, right?"

I nod.

She tears up and nods her head, too. "He's quite a kid. I wish there was more I could do, I just…" She holds her hands up in a shrug and lets them drop to her side. "I've said too much. Good luck." And she leaves through the elevator doors.

CHAPTER 45

GRANDDAD'S booming voice echoes off the walls all the way to the ER—and Granddad had been moved far out of the ER last night.

After Angela with a W. had cleaned me up and Steri-Stripped my superficial cut, she handed me a new, clean blue sling and stomped away, pointing down the hall. "Not like you'll wear it anyway. You're worse than *he* is." I can only imagine what Granddad's done in the last few hours to tick off everyone in the hospital, but there seems to be a buzz around his room.

Nurses that happily look into the rooms of all the other patients avoid Granddad's room like the plague. I pause outside when I hear voices.

"…running like squirrels all over Fallston. This has to stop Henry. Who are all these people? You know what will happen if word keeps spreading. And the will gets read for Eddie's land early next week. You gonna make it?"

"Kinda busy here, Andy. I hope to. Gotta get Jim on board."

I don't want to hear any more. I can only deal with one task at a time, and I don't give much care about Eddie's land right now. I knock gently and push open the door, surprised to see who Granddad's visitor is.

Andy Dunaway, Chief of all four of Fallston's police officers, leans in the corner behind the pink vinyl recliner, picking at his fingernails. He nods at me but doesn't smile.

"We'll have to take this up later, Mr. Andrews."

"I would expect nothing less, *Captain* Andy." Granddad looks better, but he doesn't act it. Something else is bothering him. And there's no way he could know of anything that happened in the ravine.

Yet.

He pats the bed for me to sit next to him. I hand him the phone. He studies me up and down and rubs his nose.

"Had some fun today again, Oliver?"

"Do you *really* want to know?"

Granddad wipes his brow, flips the phone open, shuts it, and puts it in the side-table drawer next to the bed.

"I expected to see you early this morning. I see you uh," he tugs at my ripped shirt, "got delayed."

Then he laughs.

Then I laugh.

What else could he have expected?

He readjusts in the bed, then says, "Let me have it. All the gory details."

I let the morning's events—from taking Margaret to the lamppost and her piano solo all the way to the fire and pale-faced stranger—spill into the room. Surprisingly, I don't break down into a helpless puddle of tears. I guess practice with drama and danger makes perfect.

Either that or I'm too tired to tear up.

"Gobsmacked. Good word," Granddad says. I can't read him. He seems as tired as I am with all the emotion flying around here lately.

"Why was Andy here?"

"Why else? More bad news. But really nothing you—"

"Need to worry about." I interrupt him and slump.

He sees my frustration. "I need to get out of here. Back to the farm. Talk some sense into Hedge's parents."

"That's just it. I don't think we have time. And you," I tap him on his forehead near the cut and he winces, "won't be able to manage. If I can get Hedge out of here somehow and down to the post, I think we can fix him. I think he's got a shot. But explaining it to the Conrads will go about as well as explaining the magic light post in the middle of nowhere to my dad."

Granddad nods. "Even if you can sneak him out, how will you get him from Fallston to the farm?"

I move to the pink recliner and put my head in my hands. Think. Think.

Where is the schemer/plotter when I need him?

Then I smile.

He's upstairs in a hospital bed. With the nicest nurse on the planet.

I grab Granddad's phone from the drawer and dial the farmhouse's landline.

Earl answers on the second ring.

"Do you think you could drive a tractor?"

CHAPTER 46

EARL HUNG up the phone and joined Margaret on the front porch where she sat in the swing, tracing the metal loops of the chain with her fingers and gazing out toward the fields. Beautiful.

In the couple of short hours since Oliver had left for town, Earl and Margaret had wonderful conversation—much of it on the piano bench —and the other of it in the fresh, albeit humid, outdoors munching on Oreos and sipping lemonade. Earl had been alarmed when they both picked up the faint smell of smoke, but Margaret insisted it had nothing to do with them and that all was right with the world.

To let it be.

And she'd crossed her arms, So he let it be.

If Earl was honest with himself, he was more scared now than he'd been the day that the EMTs had left their little Chicago house and she'd told him she was ready to die. To let her be. That fear, the fear of losing her, was a familiar friend. As was the fear of the brass-plated objects wrapped tightly and tucked against the side of the piano only a few feet away.

This current fear, though. This fear was a new stranger, and he didn't much care for strangers. The fear of the unknown. The fear of losing what he'd just gotten back. The fear of losing the future—no matter how short it would be for either of them—all over again.

"That was Oliver." Earl had readjusted his shirt tail, rolled his sleeves down and put his vest back on. Like a gentleman. Despite the heat.

"How's he doing? How's Hedge?" Margaret patted the swing next to her.

Earl sat and gazed out at the field. "Well, our young friend wants me to attach some sort of wagon buggy to their tractor, start the tractor, get the tractor out of the barn, and drive it to the end of the lane and wait for him there. Sort of a 'keep the engine running' thing it sounds like."

"Earl, do you know how to drive a tractor?" She almost whispered her question, like it was a secret. Her eyes were wide with wonder and adventure.

"That's the first thing Oliver asked me." He traced her cheek with his finger. He'd thought about all the firsts he'd had in a few short days. Travel with his wife. Farms. Chickens—chickens which were no worse for the wear, in Earl's inexperienced opinion. The ladies were happily munching on feed and clucking around their coop. The poor gal he and Oliver had put through the paces yesterday acted no differently than any of the rest of the herd. Or flock. Or gaggle. Earl wasn't sure.

He smoothed his vest and straightened his snow-white beard. He turned to face her. To watch head-on the sparkle in her eyes. He leaned his forehead against hers. "No. No, I do *not* know how to drive a tractor."

Margaret swung her feet back and forth under the swing like a carefree little girl, her flowered nightgown rippling around her bare ankles. She crossed her arms over her chest and shrugged coyly at Earl. "If *you're* going to drive a tractor, *I'm* going to ride along."

Earl thought about this for a moment. Then smiled.

Decision made.

CHAPTER 47

I TRY to contain my excitement—not happy excitement, mind you, but the adrenaline, here-we-go-again, life-or-death excitement that I've become all too familiar with—and step off the elevator down the hall from Hedge's room.

Around the corner I see Mr. and Mrs. Conrad, each on their phones, pacing, occasionally sitting, then pacing again.

An older lady I can't quite place sits on the sofa, bobbing her legs up and down in recognizable worry. I'm an expert in that emotion.

I ease down the hall toward Hedge's room. The once-empty neighboring room is filled with a doctor, an orderly, and Angela busying themselves with another patient. Angela catches sight of me, which is okay, and I point to Hedge's room. She nods.

When she moves away from the bed, I see Jerry Vleet, Mr. Deep Throat farmer, lying in the hospital bed hooked to a ventilator with his eyes shut. I freeze. Every one of the farmers is either dead or off the playing field. I can't help but feel like an avatar once again, that this is all some highly orchestrated scheme from some sick computer geek's mind, and we're nothing but puppets on his screen.

Hedge's room is darkened. He has as many IV lines and gadgets hooked to him—if not more—than before.

"Hey, Oliver." Angela says as she takes a squirt of hand sanitizer from the wall dispenser and enters the room.

"I need your help."

"Is something wrong with Hedge?" She catches herself and how silly that statement is, considering. "I mean, something new?"

"No. But I don't think anything is working. I don't think dragging him to Chicago will work either." I stand over his bed, studying the intricate tangle of wires and tubes.

Her pale green eyes tear up again. She glances toward the hall, in the direction of Jerry's room. "I don't think so, either." She closes the door behind her and lowers her voice. "I've seen this before. A long time ago."

I jerk up to look her straight in the face. "What are you talking about?"

"My grandfather. Frank."

"Granddad's Frank. Wait. You're related to old Frank?" I'm so weary and hyper focused on Hedge that some of what she says goes over my head. I can't quite picture how things fit with this nurse *and* try to puzzle out how I'm going to take Hedge to the farm.

She nods. "Everyone said he died of cancer, but I remember hushed conversations when I was home from college. And I remember my mom talking about some weird marks on his back and hands." She gently rolled Hedge slightly on his side. "Marks like this."

"I need your help. I think I can fix him or at least buy him time, but we've got to hurry." I hear myself say the words. It's like someone else is talking for me. I would never have pleaded with an adult like this before last week. That Oliver was nonconfrontational, backward, and shy. This Oliver is prepared to do anything. Two people fighting over my brain. Again.

She glances at me sideways, but she doesn't dismiss me entirely. I can tell she's listening.

"Please. I know what did this. I've seen how it happens. I think you know, too." I let some of the details of my plan roll out.

Her eyes widen, she shakes her head "no," and she wipes her tears on her sleeve. I deflate.

"What you're proposing won't quite work. I have a better idea."

Angela begrudgingly buys into parts of my shaky plan in exchange for me buying into parts of hers. This escapade is so awful that it makes my field trip scheme look like it was crafted by the CIA. "He has to go to X-ray to rule out pneumonia before they transport him and —oh." She catches herself again, and realization spreads across her face. "I could get fired. I could get fired for talking to you about his care at all, let alone what I'm thinking about doing."

"Please, Angela. I know what you're risking. But please help me get him moved."

Hedge doesn't flinch the whole time we mess with his EKG leads and machines or anything else we do to get him unhooked and ready for travel. According to Angela, nothing he's hooked to is keeping him alive at the moment. Comfortable, maybe, with pain meds and antibiotics, but those things aren't working to sustain life. Just a deep sleep and, perhaps, buying a bit of time.

Time seems to be an expensive luxury these days.

She nods and holds up the edge of Hedge's sheet for me to crawl under his bed. It's a tighter squeeze than I like, the Steri-Strips pull from my shoulder and my fresh blue sling catches on the bed's lift mechanism. I ignore the pain, in my arms and in my gut, along with the sudden urge to pee, and tuck in tight. She covers the bed with another sheet.

I feel her move the bed to the hallway and hear her pull the new "clean" bed (should anyone ask) back to Hedge's room to fill the spot. I feel Hedge and me being wheeled down the hall. It seems like we're going the wrong direction to get to X-ray, or more specifically, to the back loading dock, but then I remember Hedge saying something about this building having two elevators.

We're going out the back.

I hear elevator doors slide shut.

"He looks awful," an unfamiliar voice asks. "Oh, is this that kid?"

"Yes." Angela keeps her poise. "Taking him to X-ray for final films. He's transferring."

"Oh, good. Maybe the city docs can help. You need a hand?" The voice is kind, soft, also female. I hold my breath and pray Angela can wave off this good Samaritan.

"No. I've got it. No worries." I exhale into my armpit, the loudest exhale in the universe. Earl can hear it all the way to the farm.

"Page me if you need anything." I hear the doors slide open and I catch a glimpse of pale green scrub pants punctuated by tennis shoes with hot pink laces walking away from our direction.

I feel the bumps of a doorway threshold and almost yelp when my new wound scrapes against the underside of Hedge's bed. The sheet starts to billow, and the rush of humidity and heat tell me we've reached the dock. I hope Hedge isn't in pain as we bump along the cement. I know I am.

Angela whispers loudly as I feel the bed tilt and I get a little dizzy from the excitement and slight disorientation from under the sheet. "I'm parked just ahead. We've gotta be quick."

We'd unhooked everything back in the ICU room. The IV pole attached to the head of the bed and the monitors were for show for the transport to X-ray. Underneath the façade of tubes and wires, Hedge is free as a bird, wrapped in two hospital gowns.

I roll from under the bed. Angela already has her minivan's sliding door open. I hop in and wait until she lines the bed up as close to the door as possible. We tug and pull until Hedge lays in my lap across the middle bench seat of the van. Even with all his lost pounds, lifting him in totally limp had been no small task with my sore arms and Angela's slight frame and awkward position between the bed and the side of the vehicle.

She slides the door shut and nearly runs the bed back, pushing it up the incline of the loading dock and back into the hospital.

"It's gonna be okay, buddy. It'll be okay. Almost there." I lie. To him and to myself. I have no idea if it's going to be okay. Angela and I could be in jail by morning and Hedge could be, well…

Angela sprints back to the van and slides into the driver's seat. "How far? Wait. That's a stupid question. I know where Henry lives, catty-corner to Grandpa's place."

I adjust under Hedge's wobbling head. "About a mile. Don't get pulled over. Chief Dunaway was just here. And, hey. I really appreciate this. I know you could get into a lot of trouble."

Angela looks at us in the rearview mirror as she starts the engine. "I'm not just doing this for you. I think my grandfather would've wanted me to help."

It finally clicks. Granddad's farmer friend. Frank York. Angela York.

Angela with a Y.

I look down at Hedge and whisper, "Glad you told me about her, buddy. We got the right Angela."

She steers out of the parking lot and we head for the farm with my dying friend in my lap.

I sure hope Earl is as clever as I think he is.

CHAPTER 48

ONLY A COUPLE of hours had slipped away since Knox's grand discovery. It took him quite a while to process what he'd discovered in Oliver's grandfather's phone.

He sat in his black car parked down the road from the Andrews' farm, windows all rolled down, had a smoke, and finished off the bottled water Oliver so graciously handed over. He wished he'd had a photo of the boy's face when he saw Knox's face. If Knox hadn't walked away, Oliver was surely ready to turn on his heels and sprint to town.

Knox didn't mind that Oliver had seen him. That was the original plan, after all. To introduce himself. But Knox changed his carefully orchestrated plan midstream when the ancestral glory rained down on him at the ravine, opening a whole new world of possibilities.

With a simple ten-digit number.

A number he'd memorized at the insistence of his dying father.

The number of someone safe, should Knox ever need refuge. The number of someone who understood the generations-long burden Knox's family had borne for centuries.

A number that had come to mind, quite frankly, a day or two before when he first entertained the thought of taking Oliver on as a protégé. Oliver would also need this number someday.

Maybe some day soon.

Knox tilted the seat back and felt the humidity swallow him whole. He was tired physically from all the stakeouts and running all over this god-forsaken county, and he wanted to rest. Under the lamp post. For the rest of his eternity.

But things were happening quickly, and he'd promised to call Billy. Not that he cared about keeping his promises.

Not that he cared about Billy.

Knox flipped the seat back upright. Billy needed to be done away with once and for all. He was too simple-minded and narrow of focus to be of any practical use for Knox. Only out for himself.

What Knox was doing though, was for the greater good of all those who'd suffered at the unforgiving words and actions of people who didn't understand his kind. Oliver would be able to see this. To understand. Someday.

Oliver was a weak one, so he could be made to understand because Oliver has experienced suffering. And at the hands of Billy, he'd suffered more than enough to understand how Knox and Knox's ancestors suffered through the years.

Knox ran his hand over the laptop's keyboard. He had two lists tucked away in the deepest recesses of its files. One list he'd created with his father and slowly added to it as Knox gained more abilities. This first list contained the names and last-known locations of artifacts and bronze plates. And the power they held.

The other list contained the names and last-known locations of people who knew anything about the artifacts. Some people were clumsy and unfortunate to have stumbled upon the artifacts. Earl. Margaret. Hedge. Others, though. Others had hurt Knox. Some sent his father to an early grave with all the poking and prodding and experimenting.

He ran a hand over his stomach, feeling the raised scars created by the probes and wires and knew exactly what his father had gone through.

Knox vowed to never go through that again. To never get caught. To be a ghost.

Some of the names on that second list were right here in this county. Well, he could delete Eddie, now.

And soon, Jerry.

A few of the names were in D.C. and Nevada. Top-secret people doing top-secret things for top-secret political or personal gain. But these other folks were not by any means the clumsy farm folks or honeymooners. They were more in the class with Billy.

When bronze plates infused with magic fall into purely human hands, disastrous consequences always followed. And then the blame game starts.

Blame the creators, when the creators, Knox's ancestors, had done their best to stay to themselves with their gears and switches and plates. Alone and at peace, minding their own affairs. The plates allowed the magic instilled within Knox's kind a place to flow to, so the buildup of magical power in a semi-human frame wouldn't be so, well, disastrous.

Knox felt the back of his neck. The scars not given to him by human hands, but by that very buildup of otherworldly energy. Energy always flows from one direction to another. Always.

Knox closed his eyes and pictured the lamp post in all its glory. The twisting vines and rotating gears. The sound of switches flipping on and off, up and down and through the bronze plating. The sparks.

The power.

It refreshed him just thinking about it. And to have a place like that glorious clearing to decompress the magic's energy pulsing through his blood and bones… Well, Knox would do anything.

But he couldn't do it alone. His father had had Knox's help. His grandfather had had his father.

Knox would soon have Oliver.

He breathed deeply, and recited the phone number over and over in his head like a mantra. He imagined giving Oliver the same number and instructing him to commit it to memory. He imagined calling the number to inform the one other single trusted human soul in the universe of his progress.

To let him know Knox had found the lamp post.

To let him know of Knox's intentions to take on young Oliver as a protégé.

And to send him an updated, shortened list of names. Knox was a ghost. And he was good at what he did.

He exited the car and stretched. He grabbed his pack from the back seat, ensuring the blue vial was tucked safely in the front pocket. After the kinks worked out of his legs and arms, he would call Billy and set a time to meet under the light pole. A time this evening when Knox would erase the big bad Billy from Oliver's life for good.

And Knox will have saved Oliver twice in one day.

CHAPTER 49

EARL HAD FIGURED out the gas tank on the old machine, the last step before trying the ignition. A machine as old—or older—than Earl himself. Creaky, cranky, rusty, and worn. Like the Earl of last week.

The Earl of today was a bit more spry, though he still needed the unfortunate assistance of his cane, which took up precious seconds he didn't know if he had to spare or not. Oliver wasn't too clear on his plan.

Earl knew how that felt. He was never clear on any of his grand plans, either. Just one bit. Then the next. Then the next.

The bit that had taken Earl longer than the others was to empty the black wagon of its contents, rakes and shovels and such, and then to figure out how to get the wagon attached firmly for what Earl guessed would be Hedge's Hail-Mary trip to the light post.

He was about to climb up to the tractor's seat when he had a thought and went to the stack of tools that he'd cleaned out of the wagon bed. He chose a couple and returned them to the wagon, tucking their long handles along the edge where they'd be out of the way, but nearby in case.

In case of what, he didn't quite know. But, bit by bit the plan forms. Until everything fits.

Or they all get arrested.

Whichever.

As he passed the coup, he imagined the chickens laughing at him as he sputtered along the gravel drive for that short distance.

Earl wasn't entirely sure what Oliver had in mind, but he'd hoped it wasn't for *Earl* to drive this beastly tractor all the way to the post. Earl didn't think he had the strength, and he'd never convince Margaret to stay behind at the house. She would balance herself on the skinny hood of the tractor like a surfer girl if it meant staying in the action.

But, a man of his word to both Oliver and Margaret, Earl would do anything to help Hedge, even it if meant throwing his own shoulder out of joint navigating the cornfield.

Margaret waited for pickup at the edge of the house. She'd brought out the folded-up wheelchair. He'd not thought of that. They might need it. Pride swelled in his chest. And pure amazement that she wasn't still in the blasted chair herself.

He fought with the parking gears, the tractor grumbling at Earl's lack of ability, and finally put the thing in park, working up quite the sweat. Margaret tucked pillows and a quilt into the dusty wagon. Earl refused to let her carry the bronze-plated telegraph, and she'd at least listened to him this time.

He went into the house to get the telegraph—both cursing and blessing under his breath the whole miserable, wonderful ordeal. And, much to his dismay, he decided to lose his vest and roll up his shirt sleeves. The heat was just too much.

When Margaret saw what he'd done, she winked at him and waved a finger. "You're going to turn into a full-blown farmer if you keep it up, Earl." He smiled back at her, shaking his head, but too out of breath to give the snarky reply he was too tired to formulate.

Once Earl was satisfied he'd gotten Margaret safely positioned in the wagon—comfortable, but far away from the telegraph stored in the opposite corner—he slowly steered the noisy tractor down the lane to the corner of the field where he and Oliver had turned off to venture into the crops with two scared chickens and then his wife.

He wrestled the parking gear again, learning from his previous mistake, and settled back in the tractor seat and exhaled deeply.

Oh, how he missed his red smoking chair.

Then Margaret sent up chatty, excited prayers while Earl kept the engine running.

CHAPTER 50

MY GUT WRENCHES as we round the S-curve past the ravine of death and near the end of our gravel lane. Angela drove carefully, and we don't pass anyone. Another quiet Saturday afternoon in Fallston. Everyone going about their merry ways, none the wiser to what disasters awaited the innocent just a mile out of town.

No one seemed to be chasing down the kidnappers, either.

Yet.

Hedge hadn't moved during the ten-minute ride. Not a wince. Not even a flicker of his eyes, so far as I could tell.

My pulse can't decide whether to slow down with relief or speed up with anticipation when I see Earl—and Margaret—waiting with the tractor.

"*Those* are your helpers?" Angela was wider-eyed at the sight of the white-haired couple than she was when I asked her to help me spring Hedge from the hospital.

I shrug. "They're tough old birds."

"Oliver, I don't think—" She stares back at Earl and Margaret.

"Listen, we don't have time and you have to get back before the hospital and Hedge's parents figure out he's not held up getting X-rayed."

"I'm gonna be so fired. And I'm to blame if this goes south. No one in a courtroom would ever believe—"

A blinding flash of the obvious strikes me from Angela's words. Blame. "What if you aren't to blame? For any of it. What if you could shift the blame to someone who deserves it?"

Angela doesn't process this. She's parking the van next to the wagon, where Margaret stays seated and Earl joins us to help move Hedge. I have to yell over the tractor's engine. "Can you guys get him in the wagon? I need something from the house." Before they can answer, I wriggle my lap away from Hedge's head and sprint as fast as I can into the house, letting the screen door slam behind me.

I scale the steps two and three at a time with new energy flowing from me that I know I'll pay for later in sore legs and a busted face if I don't slow down. I rummage through my nightstand drawer, find the tiny piece of evidence, and cram it into my pocket.

Dangerously close to blacking out from lack of oxygen and the hundredth surge of adrenaline in the last 24 hours, I take the stairs two and three down at a time and bolt out of the house back down the lane. Hedge lies across Margaret's lap in the wagon. Margaret sobs over him, running her frail hands over the marks on Hedge's neck. Earl's trying to calm her down.

I reach into my pocket and pull out Billy's Volkswagen keychain. The one I'd found under Hedge's bed. "Put this back in the room after you wipe it down. Under the bed. That's where I found it in the first place."

"But who—" Angela takes the keyring, then looks at me and says, "Never mind. I know too much already."

I hug her. I reek of woods and sweat and gas and fire and who knows what else, but I don't care. "Thank you."

She nods, hops into her van, and peels out of the drive back to the hospital.

"What was that all about?" Earl yells and wipes sweat from his and Margaret's forehead. Margaret is bathing Hedge's face, neck, and hands with a wet washcloth.

"I'm framing Billy for Hedge's kidnapping," I yell back as if it's any perfectly mundane task I perform on any perfectly mundane day. Like, "Hey, I'm going to Hedge's to play video games." Or "Hey, look. The bus is here. I'm going to school now."

Earl and Margaret stare at me. Earl tilts his head and is about to speak when Margaret raises both hands in the air, waves around the washcloth and shouts "Whoo hoo! Take that, Billy!"

Earl shakes his head in disbelief, more at Margaret's outburst than at my announcement and says, "We've got to get this circus to the post. Who, uh, who will be driving this fine piece of machinery?" He twiddles the end of his beard with a shaky hand.

I grin in spite of myself. I take off the blue sling and leave it in the grass as I pull myself up onto the green duct-taped driver's seat for the first time with the engine running. "Not Granddad."

CHAPTER 51

BILLY HAD BEEN SITTING at Darla's counter for over two hours. The old diner had aged more poorly than Granddad or any other old codger he'd seen while he'd been in town.

The high-backed padded stool he sat on was covered with what Darla hoped looked like brown leather, but it was vinyl. He could spin it a little on its chrome base, but he stopped when it started making him motion sick. The light fixtures, yellowed with age or perhaps a layer or two of chicken grease, barely lit the place. If he didn't know any better, Billy would've thought he was in a bar.

Billy wished.

He had enough cash from Knox to get a semi-decent meal of fried chicken and green beans and several refills of soda while he waited for Pale Face to call him with a meet-up time. If Billy didn't hear from him in the next hour, he'd drive to Knox's usual parking spots—the school or the clearing past the farm—and hunt him down.

He'd borrowed an ink pen and turned over his paper placemat to make a list of things he'd like to ask and things he might need for his new endeavor. He tried to doodle the lamp post around the edges of his list, but he couldn't get his sketch to look anything like the post in the field and ended up scratching over it.

He took another swig of soda and toyed with the cell phone which he'd kept next to his plate the entire time he'd been here. He didn't want to miss Knox's call and he watched impatiently as the service bars waxed and waned. The bars never dipped below two if he'd simply leave it alone. But he couldn't help himself.

Darla offered him another refill, but he was full up on the carbonation and declined. Her gaze went from his glass to the front door, where the overhead cowbell clamored loudly anytime someone walked through. Darla's brow furrowed a bit, and Billy turned to see what her concern was.

Two uniformed police officers, both vaguely familiar to him from the Oliver Years, approached the counter.

"Do you own that blue Volkswagen Beetle parked on the street?" one of the officers asked.

Billy sneered. "No. I own the one parked on the roof." He softened his attitude when the other officer moved his hand to rest on the butt of the gun hanging from his belt. "Sorry officer. Yes, that's mine. I've had too much caffeine today."

"May we see your keys?"

Billy shrugged and reached into his front pants pocket and pulled out his keys. "That's funny, I'm missing—"

"This?" The first officer held up a Volkswagen keychain.

"Yeah. That's mine."

"You'll have to come with us, please. And we'll need to see your license and vehicle registration."

"Oh no. I don't know what's going on here, but—" When Billy raised up to protest, the second officer produced a set of handcuffs and slapped them on Billy's wrists so fast and so tight that his head spun. The first officer pushed him into the counter and Billy's chest knocked over what was left of the soda all over Darla and soaked into his placemat.

Time slowed down in those seconds. He could feel the cold of the handcuffs and the pressure across his ribs from the counter. Mostly, though, he watched as the brown soda spread through the paper fibers and slowly erased his lists.

"Apologies, ma'am. Billy, you're under arrest for the kidnapping of Walter Conrad and the bodily assault of Oliver Andrews. You have the right—"

"I don't even know a Walter. You've got the wrong guy."

"—to remain silent. Anything you say—"

"That rat Oliver did this. It's his fault. It's always his fault."

"—can and will be used against you…"

Billy shut up as the officer jerked him upright from the countertop, continued reading him his rights, and marched him straight toward one of Fallston's two police cars.

CHAPTER 52

KNOX TRIED to call Billy four times, which was three times too many. Billy should've been waiting for the call. Knox fumed. Billy had either gone running scared back to the city, had wrecked his Bug into the ravine, or was already at the pole like a fool.

Knox guessed he was already at the pole.

With all the magical abilities he possessed, you'd think Knox could've seen this one coming.

He cursed himself under his breath. Maybe he did see this coming. Back on the street in front of Earl's when he'd first spotted the bully. He should've seen then. His father would've told him to stop acting the toddler and think like a grown up.

And his father would be right in this instance. When it came to Billy, Knox had acted like an impulsive three-year-old instead of the power-infused adult he was.

At any rate, Billy's fumbling did get Knox a couple of steps closer to Oliver. And Oliver was now Knox's secondary objective.

Right after acquiring an all-access pass to the lamp post.

He'd arrived at the farm, ready to lay low in the tree line and gauge where everyone was. He'd checked the tracker for Earl's sedan moments before he packed his laptop away in the backpack. The car was still here at the farm, so Knox assumed Earl and Margaret were here. Oliver should be at the hospital, grieving. According to the records he'd hacked at Fallston Memorial Hospital, Overalls hadn't been discharged yet, and Hedge was ready to be transferred to the city. Oliver surely wouldn't miss seeing his dying buddy being loaded into an ambulance and hauled away.

This pleased Knox in more than one way. He could trail Hedge later. City scenes were easier for him to navigate than humid, bug-infested thickets.

It also meant Oliver would be all the more susceptible to Knox's plan.

Billy, however, was the wild card.

He ducked into the edge of the farmhouse's tree line and slinked toward the fallen log. He scanned the house and the rest of the drive through the binoculars but saw nothing. No movement. No commotion.

Earl's car sat empty in the grass to the side of the drive.

He aimed the binoculars closer to the edge of the field and his heart sank for an instant before his pulse pounded in his ears.

A wide swath of corn rows lay trampled to the ground, green stalks bent, leaning and pointing the way with their crumpled leaves.

Pointing the way to the post.

As if something heavy had run over the ground recently. Something heavy like a tractor.

Knox ventured out of the tree line to where the crumbled path started.

Where a blue sling rested in the grass.

CHAPTER 53

I'D PAUSED the tractor for only three seconds at the edge of the field where, twice before, we'd had to park Earl's car and walk the rest of the way, dragging chickens or Margaret's wheelchair through the stalks. I didn't want to drive through the corn.

But when I'd looked back at Earl and he'd shaken his head emphatically, I knew. No way we could lug Hedge's dead weight through the corn.

So, I'd turned the wheel hard to the east in the direction of the lamp post and now I steer—or try to steer—Granddad's antique machine, his pride and joy, over the rough terrain, praying to every god everywhere that Earl's hitching job will withstand the stress and strain of lumpy ground and the weight of human cargo bouncing in the wagon, although thin and frail cargo at best.

Not to mention the brass-plated telegraph. Earl grips the wrapped artifact tightly in one hand and hangs to the edge of the black wagon with the other. Both he and Margaret slump slightly, Earl over the telegraph and Margaret over Hedge's face, to block the sharp punches of the cornstalks.

The sun is at our backs, which is a blessing, because it gives one less factor to fight. And I do thank the powers that be it's not raining or we'd surely be stuck in mud. I try not to think about the loss of crops this will cause. I don't know how many acres the smashed corn would fill if laid out side-by-side.

I try not to think about Angela and Billy and the pale-faced man and Granddad's injuries and his reaction to all of this. About the pickup in the creek bed. About me driving and the smashed crops. About Mom and Dad. I try, but it doesn't work. All thoughts careen uncontrolled in my head, one on top of the another, refusing to take appropriate turns. All at lightning speed.

I try not to think about the two people fighting inside me. One brave and fearless—like the one who kidnapped his buddy and the one who jumped on the tractor he'd never driven before. One cowardly and weak—the one who'd thrown up at the sound of *someone else* arguing and the one who'd beat the lamp post until he was red-faced and sobbing.

The one who'd given up.

I try to focus on my pain instead, hoping it will keep me grounded. Settled. Able to be that first person, the brave one, for a few more minutes. I focus on the pain in my shoulder. In my other arm. In my stomach. Always in my stomach, like a noisy, irritating neighbor you'd wish would move away and annoy someone else. But the neighbor waves and smirks whenever he sees you. Like he knows something you don't. And he'll never move away.

I focus on the deeper pain in my collar bone that never quite healed. The pain in my heart from all the brokenness and loss.

The tractor tires hit the edge of the clearing and pull me back to the present chaos.

We approach the lamp post, and I pull the tractor as closely as I can to the pole, scraping the edge of the wagon against the metal base. I look back at my passengers. Hedge hasn't moved, but Margaret has covered her ears against the screech of metal on metal.

I have trouble wrestling the gear into park, and Earl yells a direction at me over the engine. I adjust my angle and the gear finally cooperates. I kill the motor and jump down from the seat, startled that the bricks under my feet don't move. My eardrums throb from the tractor's engine, which seemed louder on this trip than any of the ones I'd taken with Granddad. We probably had it in the wrong gear. Likely stripped the whole engine. Granddad's gonna flip. I shake his enraged, wrinkled face from my mind.

"We've got to hurry," I shout. I doubt Earl's ears are any better than mine.

Earl hands me the telegraph and I sprint it over to the edge of the corn while he helps Margaret slide out from under Hedge's shoulders and out into the clearing. He escorts her to the side of the field and instructs her, firmly, to stay put. She tries to protest, but Earl crosses his arms over his chest and she quiets down.

I unwrap the telegraph from the pillowcase and hand it to Earl who kneels at the clearing's edge and readies the device. I run back to the wagon and climb over the edge. I make sure Hedge is as close as I can get him to the lamp. He's paler than when we'd loaded him into Angela's minivan. I'm adjusting his head on the pillow when I hear Earl call out, but my ears are still ringing.

I turn away from Hedge toward Earl, who is waving and pointing frantically beyond the lamp post.

I whip around to see the tops of the corn stalks moving about twenty yards away from where Earl and Margaret wait.

Someone is coming through the corn. Quickly.

I hop down from the wagon and run to Earl.

The corn tops still wave out their warning.

Ten yards.

Earl fumbles with the telegraph, nearly dropping it. The hand he'd gripped the wagon edge with is bloody with cuts.

Margaret tugs on his sleeve. "Hurry, dear."

Five yards.

"Almost ready." Earl orients the device the same way we had it when Margaret was the one under the pole.

Two yards.

Earl looks toward the waving stalks. "I think it's—"

One yard.

"Now! Do it now!" I bump Earl's hand out of the way, push down on the lever, and flip the switch.

CHAPTER 54

KNOX HAD FOLLOWED the freshly beaten path until he heard the engine die. Then, ghost that he was, he decided to veer away from the path so as not to come out right on top of Billy or Oliver, or whomever else. He wanted to watch from a distance. To gather information.

To not be that impatient toddler. Not today. There's too much at stake.

As he got closer to the clearing, he could hear voices. Not one, several. Yelling.

Oliver and a woman.

Knox quickened his pace.

The faster he walked, the more the people shouted.

They knew he was coming.

The telegraph's bronze plate sparks at our feet. I look toward the pole. The lamp post hums; we hear it all the way to the edge of the clearing.

The ground beneath vibrates like ripples in a pond to the corn's edge.

In a matter of seconds, the ripples retreat, back to the origin. Back to the pole. Bricks shake lose and pebbles bounce all around the lamp. Sparks fly from the base of the pole.

Even from the edge of the field, I can see the metal pole vibrate with energy, starting at the base and working up toward the glass shade.

I lunge toward the wagon. Toward Hedge.

I feel Earl and Margaret's protective hands, grabbing, willing me to stay with them.

I break free and step into the clearing. Onto the pebbles and brick bits that were cemented down just moments ago. Now the rocks give and move under my shoes. They pop against my shins like gravel under a tire.

Two more steps.

The lamp's glass panels tremble.

I'm knocked to my knees.

The sky glows green and everything goes bright white.

Knox reached into the front pocket of his backpack and withdrew the blue vial of liquid. He unscrewed the cap and dumped the oily contents onto his hands and wrung them together, spreading the mixture evenly. He tossed the vial down and quickened his pace.

He reached the edge of the field in time to feel the energy emanate from the pole. Energy that Knox's presence amplified.

Before everything went green with magical flare, he saw Oliver.

Oliver. Weak and frail.

Fighting against the magical current.

Fighting against himself.

Until he could fight no more and fell.

I can't see. My ears ring and I can only hear my labored panting.

But I can feel.

I feel hands on my shoulders.

Icy hands.

Then a voice. Faint, but as icy as the fingers that grip me.

"Oliver."

Knox pulled Oliver to a standing position and turned the boy around to face him. Oliver rubbed his eyes, blinded by the bright white flash of energy.

Knox spotted the old couple cowering in the corn rows, unsure of what just happened. They, too, rubbed their eyes, but they weren't as close to the source when the lamp post blasted its final spark.

He'd have to multitask.

Knox turned his attention to the lamp post, not letting go of Oliver's shoulders. An old tractor with a wagon sat underneath. A faint moan came from the bed of the wagon.

Knox grinned.

He turned back to Oliver who was looking straight at him with wild green eyes and freckles ablaze.

"Hi, Oliver." Knox tilted his head and studied the boy. "I'm Knox."

It's the man from the ravine. I weigh a thousand pounds and can't move my feet.

I look over my shoulder at Earl and Margaret. Knox's eyes follow mine and he pushes me aside, taking steps toward the old couple.

The intense sense of protection I'd had over Margaret the day they arrived at the farm returns a hundred fold. "No!"

Knox turns toward me and I scoot my feet so I'm facing my friends and the wagon, forcing this pale-faced freak to face the corn.

Earl sees what I've done and he and Margaret shuffle quickly toward the wagon. Toward Hedge.

"What do you want?" I tear up. I fight to keep the coward inside me pinned down.

"Why, Oliver. I want to help. I want to…enlighten you." He grabs my bare arms. His grip is cold and oily and he smells like potent antiseptic. Worse than the kind used in the emergency room.

Behind his ghostly stare, I see Earl trying to hoist a not-quite-limp-anymore Hedge over the edge of the wagon as Margaret steadies the wheelchair.

The stranger keeps talking. "I want to show you how all of this works. How you can be…like me."

I've no idea what he's rambling on about. Earl and Margaret have Hedge slumped in the chair.

I look back to this guy. This man who helped save me in the ravine. Saved me.

Savior.

His grip isn't so icy anymore.

"I want you to know all the sacrifices I've made to get this far. To get *us* this far. You and me, Oliver. I saved you, you know."

My friends near the edge of the field where we left the telegraph. Smoke wisps from both brass plates. Green and blue. Peaceful ribbons of smoke.

"I know what it's like to be weak. To be unappreciated. Taken for granted."

It's like he's reading my soul. He takes steps backward, forcing me to take steps forward. Toward him. Toward the lamp.

Toward the beautiful, life-giving post.

I can't see them anymore. Earl. Margaret. Hedge. They've disappeared.

I only see Knox. His face hardens when he glances over his shoulder toward the wriggling corn rows. But then it changes again. Not frustrated.

Settled. Kind.

"We can be great together, you and I."

I feel sleepy. No.

That's not right.

My muscles start to relax.

The pain in my stomach, that awful neighbor, is packing his bags and moving away.

"I got rid of so many hindrances for you, Oliver. Just for you."

Sleepy. No.

This isn't tiredness.

"You're *special*. Special like me."

This feeling. This is all-too-foreign sensation is…*peace.*

Knox looked over his shoulder and saw the backs of the couple wheeling the boy away through the corn. He looked frantically between the struggling weakling in his grip and the three getting away. But Knox decided he could overtake the threesome more easily than he could ever get Oliver to come back to the clearing, so he let them go.

And Oliver was about to give in. The wriggle and pull against Knox's hold eased with each passing second. With each passing comment that Knox planted in the boy's mind.

In his very soul.

The boy was softening, Knox could see the oil working its magic— Knox's magic—on Oliver's thoughts. There was less resistance. The walls of fear and doubt crumbled like the broken brick in the clearing. Knox tightened his grip and spun Oliver with one hand toward the lamp post.

Oliver walked willingly toward the light. Knox almost had him. A few more steps to the pole. A few more steps to complete the initiation of his protégé.

Knox takes me to the light.

I lean against the post, letting its vibrations massage my back. The pain in my stomach is gone.

The smell of antiseptic is replaced with something sweet, flowery. Peaceful.

He keeps talking. I like his voice. Soothing. Assuring.

My legs relax so much that I sit down at the base of the light. Near the brass plate. Tiny wafts of smoke still ooze from the sides. I trace it with my finger and let the smoky trails play with my hand. I look up at my friend. At Knox.

No, that's not right.

Hedge is my friend. Knox is—

Knox smiles at me and nods. "That's right. You can touch. You can feel. You can know everything there is to know. I'll teach you." He puts his pale hands on the pole high above me and lays his forehead against it, looking down to where I sit looking up at him.

The vibrations intensify. The plate becomes warm, then warmer.

Then hot.

"Just a minute, now, Oliver. Just one more minute."

But I don't mind.

Knox doesn't mind. Knox isn't scared.

Knox is my friend.

Knox was almost finished. Excitement, energy, and magic all flowing in perfect harmony from his core to his hands on the post, down to Oliver.

Then he heard it. He'd been so focused on the kid, so focused on the steps that he'd forgotten to watch his back.

Like an impulsive toddler.

He heard the old man shouting. "Oliver, run!"

Then he felt it.

Searing pain in his knees as he turned to see the old man. Earl. The frail Earl he'd stalked and spied on for all those years.

Weak Earl with his wooden walking stick now firmly planted in the backs of Knox's knees.

Knox fell to the ground, toppling over the top of Oliver.

Knocking them both free from the pole's grip.

The plate burns my hand. Blisters rise on my bare arms where the man grabbed onto me. Antiseptic burns my nostrils. Knox is on top of me. Earl is yelling.

My peace is gone.

Cobwebs and confusion fill its place.

I struggle out from under Knox as he stands and pushes Earl to the broken brick. I hear Margaret cry out from the corn rows. Earl grabs his arm and tries to back away from Knox, who's taking after the old man with a purpose now.

I kick him in the back of the leg and he turns on me.

I grab Earl's cane and wave it at Knox to keep him from charging. I take steps back toward the corn. Toward Margaret, then I pause.

I can't go that way. He'll get her.

He'll hurt her.

I can't go toward Earl for fear of drawing Knox closer to the old man.

Earl is on his feet now, but he's so unsteady that I toss his cane back to him. Knox is startled by this and can't watch us both at the same time.

I glance toward Margaret. She holds the telegraph in her skinny arms. I don't see Hedge.

I think I've lost time. Is Hedge still in the wagon? Did it work?

No. I remember the wheelchair. But did it work?

How many seconds have passed? It's too quick. I can't keep track—

Knox grabs my shoulder again, but I pull free.

"Oliver!" He yells at me and I stop. Frozen. Like I did when he called my name before. "I'm the reason you're alive."

I see Earl move away, cane steadying him, on his way to his wife.

No. Margaret had moved. She's not there. Not near the edge of the field. Where—

"I'm the reason your grandfather isn't in the way of *us* saving Hedge."

That gets my attention. "What?"

"That's right." Knox pulls in closer. "Grandpa is resting quietly so you and I can be about our business." He limps a step with me toward the pole. I don't resist.

"I'm the reason your granddad didn't stop you from bringing Hedge here today. Why *Henry* is where he is."

I shake lose, stepping closer to the end of the wagon. "Granddad's in the hospital." I look at the wagon and see white hair and the tattered edge of a nightgown underneath. Margaret. Pushing something at me.

"Yes. If he wasn't there, he'd be here and Hedge would be dead." Knox's voice deepens. Sharpens. Cuts.

I see the head of the rake scoot from under the wagon. I see the white hair and nightgown pull back out of the way. Earl's made it to the edge of the field.

"Granddad's in the hospital. Because of you?" The bits and pieces of the week's events flood my mind, again not polite enough to take turns. They flick and spark like static electricity. Clear, concise sparks.

The brakes on the pickup.

"You cut the brakes?"

Knox stops and leans against the lamp post. The post hums with his touch. Thick, dark smoke comes from the lamp's top and blue sparks spring from the plate, bouncing on the bricks.

"Of course, I didn't cut the brakes. That was all Billy. But it did get Billy off your case, now didn't it?" He picks at his fingers. His long, white, icy fingers. "Everything I do, I do to bring us closer." Knox turns and faces the pole, putting both hands on it as before, and bends over me.

More bits fall into place. More puzzle shapes, twisting and turning like clockwork gears until—

"You sent Billy after my grandfather." I say this calmly though rage builds inside me. "You hurt Granddad." I look toward the corn. Margaret tends to Earl's arm, making a rumpled sling from the torn hem of her nightgown. Her hands shake. "You hurt Earl and Margaret and Hedge." I squat, my back against the wagon, and I reach behind me for the wooden rake handle.

Knox, keeping his hands on the pole, smiles. "It was all for you, Oliver. To keep Billy out of the way. Out of *our* way." His smile fades and the eyes which I'd thought were so kind only seconds before drip rage. "*I'm* the one who saved you from the ravine, Oliver. *I* made it possible for Hedge to live."

I grip the rake tightly and ready myself. My heart thumps in my ears. In my wrists. Down to my feet.

Knox glares at me. "*I'm* the one who took care of Billy. And *I'm* the one who'll bring you *peace.*"

In one swift motion, I stand and swing the rake's metal head up and toward Knox's shoulders. "No, *I'll* bring me peace!"

My aim is off, and the rake's blunt end makes contact with the back of Knox's neck instead of his shoulders. Knox's body slumps to its knees against the pole, his face coming to a stop against the twirling and twisting vines and cogwork wheels. His arms dangle, one hand resting in the brick and pebble, one hand resting ever so slightly against the brass plate.

The pole vibrates under him. I drop the rake and run to Earl. "Quick," I point to the ground.

Earl hands me the telegraph with his good arm.

The humming from the post intensifies. I feel the rippling of the ground under my shoes.

And I flip the telegraph's switch one last time.

CHAPTER 55

Fallston's cemetery is nestled on the opposite end of town from my family's farm. The weather seems to have settled down. Hot, but appropriately hot for this time of year. By the end of next month, the oak trees that guard the graves will be all shades of reds and yellows. And I'll visit her again.

That sounds nice. *My family's farm.* And I guess I'm being selfish. After all my family has gone through, I shouldn't still be on cloud nine that Dad at least signed the papers. Papers the lawyer had drawn up to allow the land to stay in the family, but I'll inherit in a few years once I'm eighteen. Dad's name is only on there for legal purposes at the moment.

My parents still think the old farmers were pulling their legs. Or drinking bad moonshine. "All of that magic nonsense..." Dad would start then wave his hand in the air. "I've got bigger issues."

Our small group walks from the minivan to the heap of ground covered by a brown tarp. The top of the marble headstone glistens in the daylight. I look up at Granddad. He's wearing a tie. He smiles at me and wraps his arm—now totally healed—around mine. Mine isn't quite healed yet, but it's on its way. Something about not following directions and keeping it in the appropriate blue sling…

Dad and Mom decided to stay in Chicago. Near Billy's temporary home. He's trying to plea insanity, but the keychain and, come to find out, the oily DNA smudge Hedge had left on Billy's back window the day of the field trip had sealed a slam-dunk kidnapping case. The fact that Billy was ranting about magic light posts and pale-faced strangers in a court of law may actually get him a reduced sentence. Or at least a stay in a nice, clean hospital.

I tug at my shirt collar and brush dust from my pants. At least these clothes fit. The shoes too.

I'm allowed to stay on the farm with Granddad and attend Fallston for school. Another batch of papers drawn up by the same lawyer, and Granddad's now my legal guardian, for which I'll always be grateful. The every-other-week visits with my parents—who aren't together, but make an effort just for the visits—have given us more quality time together than we've had in the past few years. For several hours a month, I get the warm family fuzzies and clothes that fit, and they get to check me off their to-do list.

It's a win-win.

Hedge shuffles next to me. He walks like an old man with arthritis, but at least he's walking. His parents didn't understand why he'd thrown such a fit to come here for the funeral. Their boy was kidnapped in this town by my sick half-brother with a grudge and held hostage on the Andrews' farm. Fallston should be the last place Hedge would want to be. However, being an only child, near death *and* kidnapped, Mr. and Mrs. Conrad—who aren't together, but make an effort—tend to give Hedge anything he wants now.

Well, almost.

He wanted to stay in Fallston.

His parents didn't want anything to do with Fallston.

A pang of hurt wells up in my heart. Not the first pang of loss I've had today. And probably won't be the last.

We reach the gravesite. The minister is already there, waiting patiently. Angela with a Y and Mrs. Vleet had walked ahead of us with armfuls of fresh-cut flowers. Mr. Jerry Vleet rests a few rows over.

Earl leans wearily on his walking cane. I like that cane. Strong and steady. Like his spirit.

Like Margaret's.

The minister says his final words. They fall flat. He didn't know Margaret the way the rest of us did.

And how fortunate we were that the old couple stayed on at the farmhouse for her last few months. She'd insisted. She loved the countryside. She loved the views and fresh air. We got to know them. To help them have an adventure.

But no more trips to the clearing. Earl had crossed his arms over his chest on that one.

Granddad had been the only one to return to the clearing. He was so unsettled by what he'd seen that he wouldn't speak of it and decided to leave the tractor, wagon buggy and all, next to the post. He made me promise not to go back.

I promised. I think.

I look at him now, tearing up over his new friend's loss.

Granddad knows how Earl feels.

Hedge tears up, wiping snot on his sleeve. He'd slowly plumped up since his coma. I like him better pudgy. Margaret and Earl had taken a weekend trip to visit Hedge in Chicago before his school started. Hedge said it was the most fun he'd had all summer. They were magnetic, tough old birds.

The couple had also taken trips to neighboring counties to summer fairs and flea markets. No more brass plated objects, though. She'd bought buttons and fabric and various vintage sheet music pieces which she'd dazzle us with in the warm evenings, her hands flying over the piano keys like she was Beethoven's sister. The old piano had nearly glowed under her touch.

It's hard to tell how long Margaret would have lived without magic's evil mark, but she'd put her all into packing as much life into the weeks she had left as possible.

I look at Earl as he wipes a tear away with his handkerchief. He stuffs it back in his vest pocket and straightens his beard. He bends to pick up a rose. He smells it and feels the petals. Then he tosses it onto Margaret's casket.

The rest of us follow, tossing in flowers and saying our goodbyes.

All but Hedge.

Hedge digs into his pants pocket and pulls out a semi-smashed snack-sized packet of Oreos. Earl lets out a laugh and nods in approval as Hedge places the cookies on Margaret's headstone.

I hang back at the grave while the others head for Angela's van. I need a minute.

She'd saved Hedge's life. She'd saved my life at the pole—and perhaps countless others with her willingness to sacrifice herself.

I kneel next to the grave and trace her engraved name with my fingers. I straighten Hedge's Oreos. I close my eyes and imagine my face in her hands and hear her words of comfort and encouragement. I see her crossing her arms in defiance. I see her hands whizzing over the piano keys. I see her waving that wash rag in the air and cheering me on and telling me not to be so *blastedly gobsmacked*...

I laugh and cry at the same time.

And the tears flow freely. Not from a place of weakness, but from the depths of strength.

And I say goodbye.

EPILOGUE

"FALLSTON'S A MESS. Do you know how many hours I had to log straightening out the disaster you caused? How many mouths we have to keep shut now?" The lawyer sat back in his seat so violently, the front legs left the floor and he had to correct his position to not fall over backward.

"I know," came the weakened voice on the other end.

"Do you know how dangerous it is that you're using this number now? While things are so hot?"

"I didn't know who else to call."

The lawyer sighed. It was almost five o'clock. Almost time to drive home. To the wife. To the kids.

And to top it all off, one of his labs died over the summer. Hit by a car. He put his head in his hands and rested his elbows on the desk.

Curse it. Curse them. Curse it all.

"What do you want me to do now?"

The lawyer didn't have an answer for that. There was plenty to do. But he had to play his cards right and at the right time.

"Nothing. Stay in Chicago. Blend in if you can." He rolled his eyes at this advice. This guy couldn't blend in anywhere.

"Okay."
"And, Knox?"
"Yeah?"
"The Society found your sister."

ABOUT THE AUTHOR

Beth enjoys chucking words into sentences then standing back to see what magic—or mayhem—falls out, crafting tales in mystery, sci-fi, fantasy, and general "slice of life" fiction. She couldn't accomplish this without the help of her tutu-clad Little Miss Muse and Trudi the Concrete Office Goose, who's partial to superhero capes.

Her stories have appeared in multiple publications, including Pulphouse Fiction Magazine and Ellery Queen Mystery Magazine, and in multiple fiction anthologies. She's received several Honorable Mentions from Writers of the Future. Her lighthearted blog peeks into the writing life as she pokes fun at herself and her circus of a life.

Follow the antics of Little Miss Muse and Trudi, read Beth's blog (she might have burned down her kitchen last week), and discover the stories at bapaul.com.

NEWSLETTER SIGNUP!

Get the latest release information, author updates, and exclusive content.

Visit bapaul.com to sign up for the newsletter and receive a free exclusive short story!